The Scotch Runner

STORIES, Old and New

By Elisavietta Ritchie

Elisavietta Ritchie
April 10, 2021

Poets' Choice

BOOKS AND CHAPBOOKS

LUNATIC MOONS: INSOMNIA CANTATAS, Shelden Studios (chapbook, 2018)

TIMBOT Shelden Studios (revised edition novella-in-verse, chapbook, 2017)

HARBINGERS Poets' Choice Publishers (2017)

REFLECTIONS: POEMS ON PAINTINGS, A POET'S GALLERY Poets' Choice Publishers (2017)

BABUSHKA'S BEADS: A GEOGRPHY OF GENES Poets' Choice Publishers (2016)

GUY WIRES Poets' Choice Publishers (2015)

IN HASTE I WRITE YOU THIS NOTE: STORIES & HALF-STORIES Washington Writers' Publishing House (print: 2000, e-book 2015)

TIGER UPSTAIRS ON CONNECTICUT AVENUE Cherry Grove Collections, WordTech Communications (2013)

FEATHERS, OR, LOVE ON THE WING Shelden Studios, collaboration with artists Megan Richard & Suzanne Shelden (2013)

FROM THE ARTIST'S DEATHBED Winterhawk Press (chapbook 2012)

CORMORANT BEYOND THE COMPOST Cherry Grove Co*llections,* Word Tech Communications (2011)

REAL TOADS Black Buzzard Press (chapbook, 2008)

AWAITING PERMISSION TO LAND Cherry Grove Collections, WordTech Communications (*2006)*

THE SPIRIT OF THE WAL RUS Bright Hill Press (chapbook 2005*)*

IN HASTE I WRITE YOU THIS NOTE: STORIES & HALF-STORIES, Washington Writers' Publishing House (2000)

THE ARC OF THE STORM Signal Books (1998)

ELEGY FOR THE OTHER WOMAN: NEW & SELECTED POEMS Signal Books (1996)

WILD GARLIC: THE JOURNAL OF MARIA X. Harper Collins (novel in verse, chapbook, 1995)

A WOUND-UP CAT AND OTHER BEDTIME STORIES Palmerston Press (chapbook, 1993)

FLYING TIME: STORIES & HALF-STORIES Signal Books (1986, 1988)

THE PROBLEM WITH EDEN Armstrong State College Press, (chapbook 1985)

RAKING THE SNOW Washington Writers' Publishing House (1982)

A SHEATH OF DREAMS & OTHER GAMES Proteus Press (1976)

TIGHTENING THE CIRCLE OVER EEL COUNTRY Acropolis Books (1974)

TIMBOT The Lit Press (novella-in-verse, chapbook, first edition 1970)

Poetry Anthologies edited:

THE DOLPHIN'S ARC: Poems on Endangered Creatures of the Sea SCOP (1986)

FINDING THE NAME The Wineberry Press (1983)

Illustrations by Serena Bates

Author's photo by Clyde Henri Farnsworth

INTRODUCTION OF THE ARTISTS
About the Cover

Why this cover, a reader might well ask. The wisdom found in Serena Bates' depiction of Amun Ra, worshiped in Egypt like Zeus in Greece, makes one think of the wisdom found in the short stories presented here by Lisa Ritchie. The epiphanies she offers are perhaps slight. She doesn't offer us a solution to the problem of death and the inevitable diminution due to the aging process. But here are two things she knows: 1. We are fragile, and 2. Grace emanates from some mysterious source to help us through. She doesn't crack the shell of the human experience, does not consciously deliver the yolk within. It must be love, of course, or at least some organizing genetic principle which keeps her characters strong, determined, and moving forward in the face of what we all face. It's enough that she's given us these beautifully drawn characters in whom we can intuit grace and a compassionate brotherhood. Brava Lisa, Brava.

Lately, Poets' Choice has featured a visual artist to compliment the words of a poet or writer we are publishing. This sort of synergy benefits both artists and has become a kind of trade mark for the press. With Lisa Ritchie's new book, we are delighted to include the work of Serena Bates, a very talented local sculptor who has kindly donated her work to enhance that of Lisa Ritchie. We are delighted to have both of these talented women join us in the publication of THE SCOTCH RUNNER.

Elisavietta Ritchie

The Scotch Runner:
Stories

Poets' Choice Publishing

Poets-Choice.com

337 Kitemaug Road
Uncasville, Ct. 06382
MarathonFilm@gmail.com

Library of Congress Cataloging-in-Publication Pending

ISBN: 978--0--9972629--9--5

Rose
Material: Recycled Copper
Size: 6-8" Diameter
Color: Brown, Green or Blue patinas
Can be used for indoor or outdoor display

PERSONAL STATEMENT BY FEATURED SCULPTOR, SERENA BATES

Stories are what define my work, what drive my vision, what inspire my hands...my life. My sculptures bring those stories to life, incorporating a symbiotic mixture of ideas and visions from people around me, the environment and materials where I'm working, and that sudden burst of illumination—often coming after I'm well into the sculpting process.

This is why I am here. Whether someone loves my art or not, as long as I move them in some way with my quirkiness or storytelling, I have done my job.

Amphridite
Material: Hydrocal Plaster
Size: 14H x 10W x 12D

For Clyde Henri Farnsworth

ACKNOWLEDGEMENTS

With gratitude to the editors who published these stories individually. I have tinkered with all of them since. "Amanda:" *Still Going Strong*, 2006, anthology and university graduate school textbook, editor Amalia Weinberg;

"The Crawl Space": Ginosko Literary Journal. Issue 22 Midwinter 2018

"Beyond Laramie": *Loch Raven Review*, 2010;

"Hosiah and Mike and Sukie and Her Damned Melon": *Ar Li Jo: Arlington Literary Journal, 2014;*

"Maybe it was the Moths": *Gravity Dancers*, Gargoyle anthology, Richard Peabody, editor, © 2009 Elisavietta Ritchie;

"The One-Armed Polish Writer": *Loch Raven Review*, vol. viii, no 4, 2013;

"The Scotch Runner": *Prime Number Review 43*, January 2014;

"The Traveler Meets Her Double in the Balkans": *Little Patuxent Review*, Spring 2016;

"The Ultimate Swan Watch": *The Broadkill Review*, March 2010; *Proposipia,* 2018;

"The Red Pickup" as "The White Pickup": *Roanoke Review*, 2012.

Special thanks to Joe Ruff and Nathan Summers at Calvert Library.

TABLE OF CONTENTS

Zhen Zhen
Material: Hydrocal Plaster Ed of 25
Size: 18H x 10W x 14D

As Simple as Nobody Meeting Your Train

YOU WAIT on the platform two hours, just where they told you to wait, then search the station, buffet, the nearby street. You dare not go far, you might miss them…

No one comes. Few people in the station and, through the morning, they disperse. Another train pauses, disgorges— nothing, no one. No red cap appears to cart invisible luggage or goods. The train shrills, chugs quickly away.

You remain, alone in the station on the outskirts of an unfamiliar town. Still we wait, although we no longer know what it was that we were waiting for…

A stranger appears, speaks, you speak—He invites you to the shuttered buffet. You explain you have no local money.

Indeed you have none at all, cannot obtain because the teller would ask your passwords, credentials, and you have none of those either.

You admit you crave a cup of tea, and he wants a cup of soup, but the station buffet is locked.

"A café surely isn't far," he says, "maybe only across the tracks and a block or two farther, so unless your luggage is heavy—"

"Checked," you say, though in fact you carry no baggage. At the café at last after perhaps an mile, he orders you both

oyster stew, watercress salad, a bottle of *pouilly fumé*, and you discover shared interests in stock car racing, ancient Sumerian script, Monet…

Then because hours have passed, the café manager must lock up for the night, and the only hotel is booked up, though of course you have neither money nor credit cards, and he could be a rapist, murderer, or have six screaming children at home, you pin a note to the station door, take your chances, and your life takes a different course.

You will walk a beach where only gulls and sandpipers leave their prints at low tide.

The Ultimate Swan Watch

MUST QUICKLY hang out the wash on the line three yards from the shore—

Our cove is a swan-yard!

Feathered angels, whistling swans head south one season, north the next, pause mid-trip in our bays. Two mounds of floating snow, melting and melding, two whistling swans somersault through reflections of themselves and of the leftover scarlet, gold and cinnamon trees around the frozen shore.

They dive and wash, dive and wash, over and over, just beyond our sickle of beach. They could be teasing me to dip my toes in the icy water.

The whole cove will be bare when the winter tide retreats.

Then the swans will move out to the river, and in a few days, away.

Am I Leda wringing out not laundry but golden locks?

Could Zeus transform me to a swan? Would he bother? Before he does, I must find my car, then the road, both invisible beneath the snow.

A late start as I was reading a *New York Times* article about the phenomenon of numerous apparently perfectly healthy women in western Canada with oddly-low sexual desire…Something neither the swans nor I have so far experienced.

These two swans dive, surface, shake out and ruffle their feathers…Like those models on television writhing in pleasure as they theatrically spread the sponsor's body lotion on their thighs. Is this evident pleasure in preening tantamount to or a precursor of genuine sexual joy?

Should not anthropomorphize the behavior of two monogamous swans up-ending so only the cones of tail feathers show, then shaking out their snowy feathers.

Three large black birds land. Too big for crows: *Vultures.*

I've never seen vultures on our beach. These sniff the icy air, but for what or whom? No road kill here.

Hope there's even a road beneath the snow. No emergency, but I must get to the hospital—After hanging up the wash…

Almost beak–to-beak at the edge of the beach, the three vultures wait—for me to expire, become their breakfast? Am I tastier than swans?

Are you three big dark birds not vultures after all, but swans caught in an oil slick and desperate to wash oil from your wings? Our muddy shallows are not the way to go.

Are you black swans born in Australia, unexpectedly visiting our marsh?

Whichever, after all the foraging, your bellies must be replete. Somersaults and sexual activity on full bellies I'd not encourage. Had Leda eaten?

The New York Times article concerns a study from a sexual-disorders clinic in Vancouver. Do the women in western Canada have lower sexual desire than their sisters south of the border? Yet we all need snuggling on frozen nights. Less frequent in a cold climate could be any desire to wash sheets.

But *I* must hang these newly-washed sheets on the line if they are to dry in the stingy sun before they freeze into shrouds of ice. Meanwhile, must not spook the swans…

A hospital secretary phones: I must fill in or fill out the pro-forma forms before going under the knife. Her wingless

queries concern numbers, insurance, allergies, blood type, next-of-kin. Her last question: "Do you have final directives, a living will?"

Toe surgery could kill me, I suppose. The handsome surgeon does not know me intimately enough for grudges, but his flashy scalpel might slip from my feet, slit my throat.

My living-to-the-hilt will is: Once swans and I are replete with visual, gustatory and sexual pleasures, if we cannot insure our further survival, then let this sight of leftover scarlet, gold and cinnamon trees reflected in the cove remain our vision for eternity.

T'hell with hanging the wash. Everything and everyone will anyway freeze stiff.

May I Have Your Attention Please

MAY I HAVE—*May I have your*—

No choice but to hear out whatever.

A new chapter in my life has begun and I must adapt, albeit hard to adapt to the cascading of cans and grinding of gears of garbage and every other kind of truck skidding below this borrowed apartment. Sirens and honking are ordinary urban noises but those outdoors are interrupted by the loudspeaker indoors speaking loudly through an intercom on a inner wall: *May I have your attention*—

I'm writing with this pencil stub on the inside of a label from the defunct jar of pickles, and utilize the windowsill as a table, because these are the resources at my disposal, no desk, computer or cell phone, still I must get everything down.

Damn! Again—*May I have your attention please May I have your attention please There has been an emergency detected in this building Do not evacuate Your attention please Please remain in your apartment Only evacuate your apartment when the emergency has passed When the emergency has passed an all- clear will be announced May I ha- a- a- ve your attention please*

May Day in a three-story brick building on the wrong side of what a long-ago city council designated a river but is now a dirty stream which fish shun with the exception of the lampedoosa. Isn't the lampedousa an eel? Or at least it may resemble a snake? Yesterday I thought I glimpsed an eel down in the murky water but more likely it was a water snake.

Or is Lampedoosa some tiny island inhabited by lampooning loonies?

The Loonies of Lampedoosa/ The Loonies of Lampedoosa

The beginning of a new song to compose for when I get back on the circuit!

Meanwhile, desperate for shelter and out of cash, I'm grateful for this apartment in which to practice my arpeggios. The pounding of the storm makes it a soundproof studio.

Soon as I get my cell phone out of hock, phone, locate my old agent, he'll line up more what he calls "gigs," but I "prefer engagements." Whichever, I will get back on the circuit…

This ought to be, but realistically may not be, soon.

The bard of—why not remake myself, my career, call myself *The Bard of Brick* in honor of this building which unknowingly shelters me. What about the straw between the bricks? Do bricklayers still use straw? Or some modern concoction such as plastic, which never degrades or is it downgrades, but is or is not inflammatory?

Only evacuate your apartment when the emergency i s passed When the emergency i s passed an all- clear will be announced May I have your attention please

Last night the storm drove me to seek shelter in the doorway of this building. A well-wrapped woman, who may live in one of the apartments, buzzed her way inside but her coat tails got caught in the big entrance door. After untangling her, holding the door for her, I managed to slip behind her into the lobby.

So did the piebald alley cat. It dashed past the *NO PETS AL-LOWED* sign, through my legs, through her legs, and disappeared down some dim corridor.

From the lobby I took a right onto the ground floor…Few apartments had any pinpoint of light through any crack or spy hole. All were locked. I looped back to the stairwell, tiptoed upstairs, tried apartments on the second floor, the third…

One door stood open a crack…I peeked in: the apartment was dark, and seemed unfurnished, uninhabited. Though I've never broken in anywhere, I slipped inside, leaving the door open the same size of crack.

The rain storms on—May it drown out my arpeggios…I really need my accordion. Even a mouth organ would do…

I was once a star! Fliers and clippings attest to my successive successes, they fill the suitcase stored in an old flame's cellar, the old flame indeed old now—

True, I too am older now…All the more reason to keep in practice for when I retrieve my guitar, in time the other instruments, regain my livelihood, my laptop, my reputation.

This borrowed apartment is merely an islet in the big sea of my life…

Born on an island that belonged to another country, hearing people use words brought from other isles, soon myself moving and being moved island to island, country to country, I grew up speaking several languages.

When the music teacher in elementary school said that mine was "a magnificent young tenor voice, we must nurture it," we did, and I learned songs in several languages. As I passed through the uneven years of childhood, in adolescence my voice cracked, then dropped to a bass baritone. Meanwhile I sang in school auditoriums, choirs, bars, finally opera houses, and sometimes at private parties where hostesses fawned over me as if to show they were broad-minded in inviting someone beige to their dinner table…

I bless whatever color were those kind individuals who paid for my training and those who attended my subsequent performances… I've passed through how many ports, customs controls and checkpoints around the world…Several of my songs were hits, and audiences hummed them along with me in many a venue…

Now I am older, my voice older, my tan skin wrinkled, I lack patrons and gigs, live out the clichés *Fame is Fickle, Fame is Fleeting…*

But I remember my gardener grandfather saying, as a hurricane approached our island, "One more mow before the blow…" So I too persist. Just a matter of—

I grope along the mantelpiece of the fake-fire fireplace…A key! Into the door—It turns but doesn't release the functional whatever it is called, the little thing thrust out like a—

Most likely the key to some other apartment, some other house, some other life.

I've lived many lives in many places…Like the piebald cat from some alley, it zipped past me, then disappeared in the dim hallways beyond.

A fragrance of basil permeates this borrowed apartment…

Surely thanks to a speedy departure of whatever previous occupants, on the sill I find a drooping basil plant askew on a chipped saucer. I put the pot to the sink and refresh it.

Again the loudspeaker speaks loudly through the vents: *The emergency is now concluded The emergency is now concluded Occupants may now leave their apartments The emergency is now concluded*

Shouldn't it be "the emergency is now over" or "the testing of the emergency equipment has now been concluded" or some combination of phrases?

The piebald cat pushes the not-firmly-shut door of the apartment a few inches wider and enters. With stealth, as invaders are supposed to do… Better close the door properly, but for now let cat stay inside. I refer to the cat as *it* since no chance to check it.

The anonymous cat won't demand to know what is or has been its name or provenance. The cat only cares about shelter. How mistakenly it hopes to find something to eat…Likewise.

I grope my way to the kitchenette, find the handle to open the small fridge, and by the interior light, see one jar of *Pickles. Hot* . What food value in pickles? Do hot peppers extend the life of regular pickles? Or the life of the eater thereof as they kill germs? Do cucumber slices qualify as salad, known to extend the life of the consumer? Do hot pepper bits lurk amid the two cucumber slices I extract— Ugh! They burn my throat raw. The piebald cat will not like these…

Will I ever be able to sing or it to meow again?

Ah, way back in the clear-plastic meat-saver drawer: *paté de* something! But how old?

Need a tester, or taster, to verify this dubious liverwurst… If the cat is willing to take the first bite, determine whether the liverwurst is edible, or toxic with age—I am not yet toxic with age, merely with hunger, if one can be toxic with hunger.

I feed tidbits of liverwurst to the cat, and since it does not refuse them nor keel over, I stuff the rest into my own mouth.

I check out the cat: *female* , her sides plumper than the skinny rest of her torso, lumpier. Might I become midwife to an alley cat in our borrowed apartment? The raw material of compositions…

Invisible words hammer my skull, notes of music which would be inaudible to others, slip into my ears…To the sounds of the storm, my stiff fingers play an imaginary guitar, my feet tap the pedal of an invisible drum, and on the underside of the peeled-off label of the pickle jar, I begin to compose…

Already the sky is drier and brighter. Silence on the intercom. Voices in the hall.

Cat, please pay attention. We must vamoose from this borrowed apartment before some superintendent or cleaners come in, even new tenants. When all you have left is hope, choose hope.

Look! Sidewalks are drying, you won't get your paws wet. One sidewalk leads from our unknowingly hospitable building a few blocks to increasingly crackled cement, then to a dirt road. Muddy so we wouldn't encounter many people.

Somewhere on that road, I recall a hay barn with the requisite red roof. In there I can belt out my new songs, gradually renew my contacts.

Good venue for birthing kittens.

I'm not too old to work for the farmer, he will reward my work, if only with questionable tomatoes and overgrown squash.

And yes, anonymous cat, there is always a mouse to reward you for your labor.

Trucks load, unload, rumble on. Fire engine scream, cop car sirens squeal, then stop.

Feathers

Material: Recycled Copper
Size: 8-10" Long
Color: Brown, Green or Blue patinas
Can be used for indoor or outdoor display

The Scotch Runner

BREAKFAST SONG

Last night I slept with you.
Today I love you so
how can I bear to go
(as soon I must, I know)
to bed with ugly death
in that cold, filthy place,
to sleep there without you,
without the easy breath
and nightlong, l imblong warmth
I've grown accustomed to? —
Nobody wants to die;
tell me it is a lie!
But no, I know it's true.
It's just the common case;
there's nothing one can do.

Elizabeth Bishop's lines sashayed through Sheila's head even as she kept up polite conversation with the man beside her. "My turn to host a party Friday, but friends will bring wine, and also cider so we don't have interactions with our meds—"

"I'll bring scotch," he slurred, his injection working. "Not a whole bottle, please…" She was beginning to slur

from her injection which was also taking affect. Meanwhile since he'd just mentioned he was an environmentalist scientist, she'd mentioned the monthly gathering of her group of environmentalists, to be held at her place, but somehow she had invited him to the gathering, and he was already talking of bringing booze.

Might this new acquaintance become another alcoholic on her hands? One ex-spouse enough. "You'd be the only scotch drinker."

"Allergic to wine…I'll bring some scotch in a jam jar… like a specimen for a medical test."

Appropriate, since they were in the hospital waiting room, where a half-dozen other patients were unsuccessfully concealing jars behind tattered magazines. The hospital waiting room already smelled like—a hospital.

"Friday's party," she said, "will be a potluck gathering of birders before the Christmas Day Audubon count, when we normally kayak through various wetlands. They schedule events for the whole year… My turn to host, though now I've sold my house I have only a one-bedroom apartment in which to celebrate the looming holidays…"

Not that she expected to be celebrating much. Her feverish cheeks glowed like the strings of multicolored lights on the fake Yule tree in the waiting room. A mere year ago, Benjamin, her ex, said to her, "When you, Sheila, enter a room, you glow, the whole place glows…You will manage on your own, darling, you're enough of a femme fatale." Benjamin, from whom she had parted amicably enough—both had found other individuals to divert their attention—used to say that with   her peachy cheeks and buxom bosom, she must have stepped out of a Renoir painting, and he hung a reproduction of the lady with a parasol over the mantelpiece.

Now Sheila felt more like Edvard Munch's bony screaming female. She had seen herself in the mirror: anorexic as a Giacometti sculpture. Since she had donated most of her clothes to the local Goodwill, she wore her old jeans which used to be too tight, whatever glow was thanks to intermittent fever, and she dreaded anything to do with the word *fatale*.

So she felt far from glowing, this supposedly routine outpatient visit to the hospital for "a little procedure not worth discussing." The stranger beside her also seemed to be there for "a little procedure" he didn't want to discuss either.

"Not even an old *Time*," the man beside her said as he fished through tattered homemaking journals on the table.

"That year-old sporting magazine focuses on the best way to shoot a magnificent stag for its antlers and venison…Wish I'd brought my book but it was too heavy to lug on the bus."

"What're you reading?" he asked.

"William Least-Heat Moon's *Blue Highways* ." "Coincidence: Tom, my son, and I listened to it on a CD as we drove from Fort Bragg."

"I listen to audio-books while at my drawing board." "Fine artist?"

"Wage-earning artist. Little time to be fine." She extracted the sketch book from her canvas bag. "Forgive me, the shot is making me feel weird, but I must finish some illustrations for an ecology text, before…"

"I'm trying to finish writing an environmental text… before."Then he wrote on the back of her layout some lines from Goethe:

> *To die is to grow*
> *you are only a troubled guest*
> *on the dark earth.*

"Yes, a dark earth…" Logical, she mused, that the mutual concern for impending mortality made them philosophical. "But too soon for either of us to go! Your hair is silvering, your skin weathered like any hiker's, but you're still more-or-less young and you have great cheekbones!"

She was embarrassed to find herself indulging in such personal conversation with a stranger. The anesthesia—

"You have beautiful cheekbone, beautiful skin, beautiful hair," he said.

She didn't admit that her brown hair had silver interlopers. Hair dyes and skin crèmes did their bit to stave off the realities of time, but wrinkles and strands of white hair lurked beneath the surface. "Losing weight highlights the cheekbones…"

She unfolded the layout of another save-the-wolves newsletter overdue at the printers. She had barely lifted a pencil when they began to talk of wolves, then marine biology, other realities of the animal kingdom. "Even asleep, the fox dreams of nabbing the rabbit peacefully nibbling grass to the quick," he said. "Think what those frolicking lambs did to Australia, and our own West. As for humans here—"

A marine biologist working in estuarine ecology, Alan was completing a report on over-fishing, over-crabbing, over- oystering, and alien species in a natural environment, focusing on European green crabs and Asian oysters.

Sheila had written on Japanese starfish for her master's degree. "I'd planned further research in northern Australia... Some 'golden year.'" No need to mention that neither was expected to be around for those so-called golden years, nor that most of their projects would remain unfinished until passed on to others to complete. They agreed there was not much joy in buying a Christmas tree this year. "I've saved a few ornaments that would break if I shipped—"

A nurse called out "Ms. Sheila?" She stood up with an unexpected sob. She was horrified at her lack of self-control, but nobody paid attention except the man beside her. He stood up and touched her arm. "Camus claimed that 'one cannot appreciate one's life until one has faced one's death.'"

"I've not learned to appreciate pain."

"You'll be okay, honey," the nurse said. "They'll give you something more."

They did. Knocked her out....

***

Afterwards, Sheila couldn't remember what she and the man in the waiting room had discussed before their respective "procedures," or afterwards still woozy from anesthesia. "Doctors insist that after treatments we zombied patients waste a whole hour sitting around," he said, "to make sure nobody faints, smashes skulls, sues them...At least I have you for company, Sheila."

She didn't remember exchanging names, but searching in her purse for a comb she spotted a card: *Alan Faulkier,*

Environmental Consultant . She recalled telling him of the party on Friday for her environmentalist friends, and her despair that she would not be going on any of their spring camping trips. "Without my house anymore, I've shipped my camping gear along with whatever remaining good furniture and china to my daughters in California…"

"My house," Alan said, "is already in Tom's name. He'll be off at grad school, but could rent out the house…"

So she had inadvertently invited this stranger to the party.

Did he mention a wife? Sheila surely said the requisite, "Of course, bring her."

The nurse finally decreed them steady enough to leave. "You aren't thinking of driving yourself, honey—" the receptionist said.

"Sold my car a m-m-month ago." Sheila pulled out the bus schedule.

"Oh, post-procedural patients aren't allowed to use public transportation," the receptionist scolded. "You must have been informed that a reliable family member must drive you home."

"I've n-n-n-no 'reliable family members' around." Sheila was terribly conscious of slurring.

"But honey, you shoulda made arrangements with some friend or neighbor."

"I wouldn't trouble them…Nobody knows I'm—ill." She had gently told not only her ex-husband but her former lover that she couldn't see them again, likewise her friends, for she was going on a new adventure, let them think what they wished. Friday's party would obviously be the last with her environmentalist club.

The receptionist was about to say more, but both her phones were ringing and three buttons blinking.

The man, and at his elbow a younger man in his twenties, wearing military fatigues, followed Sheila to the receptionist's desk. "We'll get you home safely," the younger man said, glancing at her address on the chart. "It's on our way…more or less." he hooked his arms inside both their elbows and marched Sheila and the man together toward the exit. An orderly waylaid them with wheelchairs.

"Don't need them—" Sheila protested.

"Jus' sit comfortable," the orderly insisted. "Git a free ride to the entrance. Parking garage a ways over there."

"Wait here." The younger man's words reached her through the leftover fog of anesthesia. He reappeared in a muddy gray jeep, "Dad's legs are long, he's gotta be in front…" He helped Sheila from her wheelchair into the rear seat, and the older man from his wheelchair into the passenger's seat. "I don't want to trouble you—" Sheila said.

"This old Wrangler may not look like much, Ma'am, but she's has gone over a lotta rough terrain, she'll get you home on a regular city street."

While they were driving toward her brownstone apartment building, through the persistent fog she heard them discussing sniper school and how, in the wilds of Georgia, Tom (which seemed to be name of the younger man) maxed the army's training exercises, "… thanks to our hiking, bushwhacking and hunting since I was six, when you first showed me how to hold a rifle."

Had she hooked up with a couple of trigger-happy rednecks? Okay, not too late to broaden her social circles, especially in this half-drugged condition.

Pulling into the reserved parking space outside her apartment house, Tom (?) turned on his blinkers and climbed out of the jeep. The older man opened his door and half got out too, then took her hand for a long moment. "Friday, Sheila?"

"Oh…the party…Did I give you my apartment number?" She couldn't remember even having told him her name.

"Penciled on your card."

Her keys slipped from her fingers. The younger man retrieved them, took her elbow, punched to knob for the little elevator, propelled her in and rode with her two flights to her door. "Wish we could stay and look after you, ma'am, but I must settle Dad at home, and get myself to the bus station."

She was nonplussed by the repeated "ma'am." Military courtesy, of course.

"Good Christmas, Ma'am. Won't be able to return home till... what's labeled 'compassionate leave.'"

***

Sleeping all afternoon, though the painkillers still dulled her mind, she set about finishing her draft layout she'd planned to work on in the waiting room until that anonymous man diverted her into conversation she barely recalled now. She put on the kettle for strong tea.

The phone rang. "Alan Faulkier here. How do you feel?" "Oh! Fine, thanks for the ride! And you?"

"Fine, too." "Are you lying?" "A bit. Are you?" "A bit."

"And the report?" "Who knows." "You worried?"

"Too late to worry, too soon to hear." "You?"

"Too late, too soon." "Too busy." "Much."

"Me too."

"Did we talk about a party?" "Yes. Friday."

"Someone on the other line—" "Both gotta run—"

"Or better, sleep—" "We'll talk later."

They did. He phoned daily, and they talked and talked...

***

She had no interest or energy to do much before the long- promised holiday party. Her house sold, the heavy furniture already distributed, she rented month-by-month this one- bedroom walk-up, where brown, cream and white constituted the interior decorators' full palette. Fake-oak panels along every wall, brown cabinets, window frames curdled-cream, wall-to- wall carpet mottled brown, dull-yellow and off-white, sofa in brown-gold plaid, a dirty-gold Lazy Boy. The kitchen floor had brown-and-beige patterned squares. "Useful for hiding dirt," the manager had remarked. Batik shawls she had bought on a long-ago trip to India were also useful for covering the worn couch and armchairs.

Nothing seemed useful against the ants, but they were nonetheless interesting creatures and the small size.

On the next Friday noon a florist's deliveryman buzzed. "Sorry, wrong address," Sheila said through the intercom, "I didn't order anything." The delivery man insisted, and two minutes later knocked on her door. When she unwrapped the green-and-silver striped paper, the fragrance of earth filtered throughout her two small rooms. She extricated a magenta fuchsia plant. The florist's card read "*From Alan. Perhaps this can serve as a Christmas tree.*"

She hung her few leftover ornaments on the branches, then quickly tidied the apartment, though little to tidy. She'd already given her ex-husband the Renoir print, along with most of the CDs. Most of the furniture, china plates and glasses she had already shipped to her daughters in California: Tillie had an apartment, Molly was leaving the dorm to find one.

Sheila quickly threw an Indian batik over the kitchen table, then put on her black lace bra, black lace panties and slip and pulled on her one remaining dress, black velvet, black fishnet stockings, and spike-heeled imitation Prada sandals. No point in saving these for her funeral: she'd leave advance instructions with the local morticians to clothe her corpse in these, at the least to give whatever mourners a kick.

The buzzer rang, soon followed by a knock on the door.

Alan carried in a knapsack and boots, explaining, "My plans depend on the tide table, so before dawn I'm heading to a cabin on the Bay, a future legacy from my Uncle Rob, now 92."

How soon will the cabin become Tom's legacy, Sheila wondered. How far along was Alan?

He studied her as he hung his parka on a peg. "You look spectacular!"

She hardly felt 'spectacular.' But at the ensuing party, there would be no talk of illness or death.

He extracted from his knapsack a recycled mayonnaise jar of what he murmured was Chivas Regal, followed by tins of smoked oysters, caviar, jams, smoked salmon, artichoke hearts and Swiss chocolates. "His last visit, Tom filled my cupboard with this bachelor fare I don't feel like eating alone."

The wife Alan had mentioned at the doctors' offices turned out to be in the context of, "My wife didn't like roughing it, but parties, yes…Off to whatever heaven five years ago, and yes, fortunately she believed in heaven and was philosophical about death."

"I'd like to hope for some sort of a heaven," Sheila said. "I'm not philosophical about early departure from an earth I'm still working to save, along with its creatures. Shouldn't we return their earth to some semblance of a more peaceable kingdom?"

"Peaceable kingdom? Every critter is out to kill another."

The buzzer buzzed, then a few minutes later, buzzed again, then again. As they trooped in with their wine, salads, casseroles, cookies and paper plates, several friends whistled. Nothing to whistle about here, though obviously she was not going to bring up—her personal realities. Enough that her one remaining elegant outfit did its best to hide her now bony body. A couple of old friends mentioned she looked "a bit wan these days, but congratulations on whatever your diet plan."

"Hey, your apartment isn't as bad as you described it!" "A bit dark, yes, but you can keep those venetian blinds open."

***

After the potluck dinner, people began packing up their casserole dishes and filtering away, each with a holiday present from Sheila. She gave the guest who was a lepidopterist a perfect Luna moth she'd caught in Brazil and framed. For an archaeologist, the trowel she'd used in Jordan. Vases, platters, books for others, and her umbrella stand full of dried cattails to a lawyer for his office. Distributing her expendable possessions continued to be simple as watching petals fall from an overripe peony. She was shedding *things* .

"We'll pick fresh cattails tomorrow," Alan said.

Why the "we," she mused, glad no one had asked for the new plant, which she did not intend to give away anyway. What hand-me-down for Alan? He obviously had no need of *things* , and had read most of the books remaining on her shelf. She handed him her tape of Dylan Thomas reading his poems, including *"Do not go gentle into that good night… Rage, rage, against the dying of the light. "*

She slipped the CD with the Bach fugue on the player.

Alan was already carrying used paper plates to the trash basket.

Afterwards he embraced her in the usual farewell-and- thanks-so-much-for-the-nice-party hug. The hug, however, lasted. Then he opened his knapsack, extracted a little travel toothbrush, and slipped into the bathroom. She slipped a painkiller in her mouth before she brushed her teeth. A few minutes later, wordless, and as hosts not having drunk a drop of the bottles of wine or of Alan' jar of scotch, she carried a blanket to the couch but as it was too short for his long legs, she showed him to the bed and planned to curl up on the couch herself. But somehow both fell into her bed half-clothed, managing only desultory cuddling before falling asleep.

She awoke several times with this near-stranger curled tightly around her. Suppose the "procedures" were merely pro- forma, the doctors had miscalculated and misled him, and he died in her bed this very night? Or she? Neither was yet, surely, that terminal. She hated the word. Years ago, her mother spoke of an aunt's diagnosis, and Sheila age thirteen had retorted, "But we're all 'terminal,' Mom, aren't we?"

No side-stepping around the word now. The artistic renderings of Death with his thoughtless scythe had to be upgraded to reality.

Half asleep, she heard Alan sigh, felt his fingers smoothing her hair, then fell asleep again. She awoke after sunrise on hearing both daughters' voices in the process of recording on her answering machine. Anyone else she might have ignored.

"Guess what, Mom! Big news!" Tillie said. "Hop a plane to Cozumel for Christmas week! Martin's parents are renting a villa for a family reunion—perfect time for us to get married!"

"Wonderful!" Sheila said.

"We gotta discuss what you gotta do for the reception—" "I'm bringing Jonah," Molly broke in, "all of us will be in the wedding."

"Why don't you two get married too?"

"Strange you suggest that," Molly said. "But we're waiting till after graduation."

"Don't wait," Sheila said, "if Jonah is really it, seize the day…"

"Since when were you so impulsive, Ma?" Tillie asked. "We're living together weekends," Molly said. "Sorry, Ma, to shock you."

"'Course not. Just that by June—" She paused. "I may be on a journey…" She'd not intended to relay her own news until the last, so to speak, minute. Afterwards the family lawyer could fax copies of her already signed will, mail letters she must get to writing. Meanwhile, she'd not spoil her daughters' happiness. "June is far away. Seize the day."

"Still a bit uncertain…Jonah and I have different temperaments, interests…We need time out in the world…"

"Then, Molly dear, wait…I've met a young man you might like. Working toward a Ph D. in ecology, I think.…Yes. Mountain climber and canoeist like you…Currently a first lieutenant about to be shipped overseas. He might like a pen pal—though probably has plenty of girls writing him… Apparently not…Oh, here's his APO address…So, if you can fit more distractions into your life—"

"Sure, and give him my address. Hey, who's there feeding you information?"

"Ummm…well…his father…" "At this hour? *Mother*!"

"Yes, dear."

"'It's okay, Ma. Seize the day and a plane reservation right away while you can get flights cheaper. Check the Internet—"

"I'll…I'll try to come…"

"Only try, for heaven's sake? Ma! Of course you'll come.

We'll be fancy. I've bought a gorgeous organdy. Bring your blue silk cocktail dress, a perfect mother-of-the-bride outfit."

"I'd have to find something new. I've lost weight." "Lucky you!" The girls said in unison.

"I'll be shipping more stuff for both your households, the rest of the silver and china, so wait before buying anything."

"You redecorating?"

"Reordering my environment. A craving for space… Anyway, here's to lovely weddings, great futures. I'll check what flights…"

She hung up and lay back in bed. Alan hugged her. "So you want to be mother of two brides at once?"

"Gotta pack it in, as the girls would say."

Yet would she be up to the trip, all the ritual festivities?

Catching cross-country flights daunting now…

"I'll drive you to the airport," Alan said, "as long as you'll be back in a week."

She leaned over and kissed his brow.

Alan surely had several lady friends. This—one-night stand— would remain technically what her mother would call "a platonic relationship even if Plato…"

Alan pulled her toward him, fingering her black lace slip. Then overhead, neighbors began their day with loud rock and children rampaging like elephants. "What I hate about apartments," both grumbled simultaneously. Sheila expected him to make apologies and take off.

"Might I shower," he asked, "unless you want to be first?" "Clean towels on the rack. Waffles in the freezer…Tea?

Coffee?"

"Tea's fine. Tom found our old waffle iron, but I don't lay in supplies of waffle mix. Sometime I'll make some for you…."

She didn't want to ask if Alan made waffles for all the lady friends he surely had, nor did she want him to ask about the gentlemen friends she had, or had had…

"With that damned noise upstairs," Alan said, "let's get the hell on the road. Yes: both…The cabin's in a marsh near some tributary, I remember from childhood visits, but must recheck maps…Uncle Rob owns the cabin with several old-boy hunting and fishing buddies, but nobody there this weekend.

He swears it's in good condition. If we can find it."

Preparing to head into the mid-December drizzle, she pulled on blue sweatpants and sweatshirt over long black silk underwear. They filled their backpacks with extra socks, party leftovers and the jam jar of scotch he'd neglected to open as well as his unopened tins of hors d'oeuvres. She packed two cans of protein drinks. Appetites might return, and energy.

Tossing packs and parkas into the jeep, they set out.

"Tom might enjoy corresponding with your Molly," he said as they wound out of city traffic.

"Regardless whatever you've told him about your condition, don't mention anything about—mine," Sheila urged. "Just so the news doesn't reach my girls. I've only mentioned I'm working against the clock to finish articles…Must get as far along as I can on Australian green crabs…"

"I've always wanted to check out Australia," he said. The Metropolitan Opera matinee came on the radio:

Tristan und Iseult . At the entre-acte he said, "Let's skip ill-fated lovers for a while." He slipped the Dylan Thomas disc into the CD player, replayed *"Do Not Go Gentle into That Good Night. "*

They left highways and secondary roads, turned onto a dirt road through scrub pines and bayberry bushes, and parked.

"Can only hope this is the right place," Alan said. "May be farther downriver. Anyway, we'll have to get there before high tide, or turn back."

He dug wading boots out of the trunk, passed the smaller pair to Sheila. Amazing he has a pair to fit me—Of course, his late wife's boots or a lady friend's.

They set off through the spongy tufts of eelgrass and cattails around a marsh. Fragrance of swamp and rain despite the cold. Several Vs of geese flew overhead. "Strange angels,"

Sheila said, "celestial hounds."

Deer cantered across their path, unseasonable mosquitoes buzzed around them, as they walked in a semi-circle around the marshes, to a cove full of small diving ducks, white with jet black heads. "And those—" he pointed with his binoculars beyond the diving ducks, to a dozen coots. "those are eiders."

Rain began in earnest, drops trickling through the neck of her parka. Her pack grew heavier, fatigue draining her veins.

The wading boots rubbed blisters: Was the ghost of their previous owner taking revenge? Ghosts of late wives could be fearsome…

The boots turned out to be the legacy not of Alan's late wife, who "had not liked mucking around in marshes," but of a male graduate student returned to California to study desert terrapins.

Tide was filling low ground higher, cutting off the path. "With a full moon, neap tide," Alan said, "ridiculous if we let ourselves get caught…"

"Should we try a short cut along the river?"

This seemed to be a mistake, or was it? They came flush against a high chain-link fence, and followed it through clusters of scraggly cedar trees. Behind the fence they saw a cabin and a ramshackle pier. A heron on a piling flapped away with guttural croaks. He didn't have a right key for the padlock: the only option was to climb the fence. "How to fit these boots between the links—" He took out a Swiss army knife, and pried the thick wires holding the fencing to the top rail. Then he unraveled the wire enough to pull the sides apart and create of a gap for them to scramble through. "I once taught science in a rough neighborhood," he explained. "The boys taught me."

Some were juvenile delinquents who broke into parking lots…

She couldn't admit her fear of heights, but somehow managed to climb the rest of the way.

The wooden cabin was set on cinderblocks three feet from the ground. Two boat trailers held skiffs under tarpaulins.

Plastic floats hung down from an airy architecture of chicken-wire crab pots stacked against the back wall. They searched under the eaves and steps for a key. No luck. The windows were shuttered, small and too high.

"Might your uncle's buddies turn up to use this cabin?" she asked uneasily. "With AK47s bristling..."

"Shooting seasons are staggered, this is a dark week."

Remarking again about skills learned while teaching, Alan slid a plastic credit card into the lock and managed to force the spring bolt back. He pushed open the door, dislodging spider webs and dust. They set down their packs on the wooden floor. "Thank God for scotch," he said. "Will you break down and have a sip?"

"Not quite yet," she said, her teeth chattering.

Perching on a box that held duck decoys, they took off their wet boots and sopping socks, and in the dim light looked around. A green canoe on its side, crab nets, a frazzled broom, pairs of oars and paddles, bags of decoys, several canvas cots folded against another wall. Coleman lanterns—a gentle shake proved little fuel left.

Alan produced his key ring holding a small penlight. "No telling how long these silly things—My big flashlight is dumbly back in the jeep, along with the rest of the bottle of Chivas Regal. But have a sip—"

"Thanks...I don't usually..."

"Supposedly a painkiller...Maybe helps focus on life." Life jackets hung on the walls—As if. But as if by tacit agreement, neither mentioned illness anymore. Her present

pain was focused on her heels. She hung her wet socks over the canoe's gunwales, and inspected her blisters. He extracted a small plastic pouch from his backpack, and taking her cold feet into his lap, dressed them with ointment and Band-Aids. Then he rubbed her feet until the warmth flowed upward, and pulled up her dry pair of socks. Her tears welled at his simple gestures.

"Even when the tide ebbs, we'd have trouble making it back to civilization before dark," he was saying. "At daybreak we can follow the tire tracks out back, they'd eventually take us to the jeep. Does either of us have pressing engagements?" "Only work. Christmas shopping…"

"Sent everyone subscriptions to *National Geographic.* I took Tom to my broker's—haven't much of a portfolio, especially after putting him through university—but at regular intervals money goes into his account toward his master's degree. GI Bill should help. The latest Sci-Fi paperbacks are being sent to his APO address. Ditto subscriptions to geology and geophysics journals, to give him a start before he returns."

"You really are—" she was about to say, preparing to die, instead managed "organized."

"Learning to be practical."

They looked around for a stove. Only a hibachi in the fireplace. "Those Coleman lamps are low in fuels," he said, shaking them. "But even after lamps were invented, people went to sleep at sunset…" He stood in the doorway shaking tarpaulins and blankets free of insects and dust. Curtains of water began to pour from the roof. "Better eat while we can still see the food."

She spread the dishtowel tucked in her pack, and, hands shaking from the cold, arranged smoked salmon and cream cheese on the bread. "We forgot cups…"

"Our germs are environmentally-friendly, and scotch is germicidal. Should be better for the heart even than red wine."

"How's your heart?"

"Thawing after a long sojourn in the freezer. Like your waffles. Your heart?"

She wanted to say, *Thaw mine too, please, something light-hearted, flirtatious.* But her mouth was full of smoked salmon…

How can one know the inner l i f e even of those with whom one spends much of a lifetime. And here we are, literally strangers, knowing that we know each other deeply. The way hanging supposedly focuses the mind, so the impending–imposing—limiting— Clichéd thoughts, but...

"We can boil rainwater over that hibachi…" Alan was wiping out a pot. "Tea bags in my pack. We'll test a few inches of scotch. Need some to warm you now?"

"Just you," she said, surprised at her own directness.

This time his mouth was full of smoked salmon. He passed her the scotch. "We'll save the tea for breakfast."

***

At first light, the pier was paper-thin, as if stretched between pencil shafts over foil. A heron alighted on a stick. Only with sun would anything assume substance. For now the shore remained dim, undefined.

When they finally reached her apartment, they threw muddy clothes into her washer-dryer, showered, heated soup, and toasted with the last inch of the scotch they'd never got around to drinking.

They Googled time tables for flights to Los Angeles and thence to Brisbane, made reservations, and rented a jeep to explore the rain forests. No need to say: *We will die with our rain boots on.*

Sorting the clean laundry, their socks, shirts, underpants and sweatpants entangled with each other, she burst into tears.

"What's wrong?" Alan asked in alarm. "Pain?" "It's only—I'm so happy—to have met you—"

"We will not go gentle into any night," he said, "but utilize every hour until dusk." He scooped her up, and carried her to bed.

Maternal Instinct
Material: Raku Fired Ceramic
Size: 5H × 10W x 14L

The Polish-Canadian Financier Invites Me

My story of the one-armed Pole? Yes, you being from Warsaw, might be interested. Shouldn't we order first? You're a marvelous host, this Toronto restaurant is elegant, but the waiter just gave us menus and everyone's hungry. Maybe after the Vichyssoise…

Doubt Jerzy could have afforded this restaurant on his brief trip to Toronto as an official, almost-trustworthy, writer from Poland here for an international conference…a useful excuse to travel beyond the Iron Curtain countries.

Not been back? You had enough trouble under the Nazis, and now the Communists would—They imprisoned you for a poem? In this hemisphere, poets aren't that important.

Pheasant?

Yes…Picnicking beside the Danube between lectures at the writers festival, we pretended the ubiquitous sausage was pheasant…Allowed little foreign currency, most Blokniks brought in their food to the convention. Jerzy kissed the coarse Polish bread before cutting… He was somehow enough acceptable to the regime to be permitted to travel to nearby meetings where most attendees were likewise from "fraternal socialist republics."

Oh, me? I merely happened to be alone in Belgrade to give poetry readings at some university English classes and one at an international literary conference…My own encounters?

Adventures? Harder to tell true stories than invent…But your other guests want to discuss monetary crises, transnational pipelines, gold prices!…

Madame Someone across the table is relating how a cat slid off a slanted roof sixty stories up, spread himself out to slow the descent, landed on four feet, and walked away albeit unsteadily. If fallen from only two stories—splat.

Important discussions buzz around us, about monetary crises, international agreements, politics in the so-called Third World…

My "pheasant" is a quail which the dab of truffle sauce can't moisten…

Hard to talk across this large circular table, on both sides five people between the host and myself. Complex geometry.

Perhaps distance is useful: pain through the other end of a telescope shrinks to a pinprick…Lovely wine! One drop is enough for me! Must keep my head!

Jerzy cherished every sip of wine and life outside Poland.

He knew his vintages…The cost of this bottle would feed people over there for a week. Thank goodness you're paying— I'm not so gauche as to say so…You're kindly and courtly as he, but more handsome, especially in your pinstripe suit, striped tie. Even wearing a suit, or jeans, his plaid scarf wound three times around like a French intellectual, Jerzy still looked the prototype Polish peasant. But not the typical "socialist cultural officials" allowed to travel abroad, they were squeezed into shiny western business suits, several actually ate peas from a knife. They snuck off to buy Japanese electronics and girlie magazines, downed what vodka they could bring in, plus whatever vodka, wine and whiskey our hosts offered.

Jerzy didn't swill away like the others. His manners showed he was of the nobility. *Szlachta* , you say? Like other older educated Poles and Russians I encountered, he spoke French, our common language, Russian words thrown in…My family's province of origin? My father traced our family to fourteenth-century estates in a part of Poland that occasionally became Russian. Possibly Jerzy and I share ancestral blood?

You warn Jerzy could have belonged to the Polish KGB. Only official Blokniks and 'safe' cultural types, whose families remain at home, are allowed to travel abroad, accompanied by vigilant *nyanushkas* —minders, watchdogs, officials of the Writers' Unions— to make sure they don't defect.

No, two other men in that foursome of Poles were the *nyanushkas* —Jerzy could smell them in any East Bloc delegation. Yet I wonder if these Polish official writers, like their counterparts in the Soviet Writers' Union, wrote much

literature. More likely pro-forma reports, and denunciations of their colleagues....

Three enormous Soviet Writers' Union *nyanushkas* constantly shepherded the skimpy Russian poet, who shyly recited his "safe" apolitical verses about birches, blizzards and brotherhood-among-peoples. One Soviet *nyanushka* brought out a guitar, and sang of moonlit nights—*i notch takaya lunaya* . I grew up on those old pre-Revolution folksongs. Nothing like Russian folksongs to subvert, co-opt, seduce.

When our special Writers' Bus stopped at a mountain café for lunch, the Soviet *nyanushkas* sang, drank, ate and fell asleep in the café. The Russian poet slipped outdoors to talk with me under the grape arbor...

When our own mixed group of some dozen writers picnicked by the Danube in the late September sunshine, the Blokniks brought out hunks of fresh French bread they'd filched from the hotel's break-fast baskets as well as the last of their stale bread and sausages carried from home—they must avoid spending their few precious bills of foreign currency.

From my backpack I extracted the duty-free Scotch I'd bought at Frankfurt airport, and cups of tin, plastic and paper quickly ma-terialized. After lunch the Polish *nyanushkas* stretched out on the grass and, hats over faces, snored. Jerzy and I had drunk only apple juice, and slipped off to wander the riverbank. He talked more freely...

He spoke of midnight knocks on the doors of childhood: early during the Nazi Occupation, his parents out queuing for whatever they could find in the stores, Jerzy remained at home with mumps. He opened the apartment door: Nazi officers! But they noticed his swollen jowls, and fled.

Another nocturnal visit: Polish officers in civilian clothes, heading for the USSR to help fight the Nazi invaders, paused for his mother's cabbage soup while Jerzy's father packed his knapsack, kissed his wife and son, departed with the men…

Another midnight, six Soviet soldiers appeared at the door and instructed Jerzy and his mother: "Pack your warmest clothes for camp." In his suitcase Jerzy tucked an inkwell. By the time the train reached the Russian border, everything was purple…Camp did not mean children's games. His mother disappeared…No sign of his father…

Yes, I know the Soviets shot several thousand Polish officers in Katyn Forest….

Toward the end of the war, Jerzy managed to escape with a carful of Poles to Persia. In a car crash he lost his arm at the shoulder, in Turkey, his innocence. Back in Poland after the war, he expected heaven…

No, we didn't discuss politics. No need. And the hotel and cafes were undoubtedly bugged: a few words overheard could get one into trouble. Communication through eyes and skin is safest. *Sous- entendu.*

Oh yes, we saw the Polish countryside! First we all piled into the Writers' Bus and attended Babels of readings, lectures, museums. Then the Bus took us into the countryside, where pumpkins and cabbages lolled on the fields. We dipped our toes in River Drina, visited monasteries and local museums.

Our Serbian guide, who'd taken the seat beside me, as if scripted, constantly recited Communist dogma.

Yet when we stopped to visit an old Orthodox church, he suddenly sang mass! How could he have known it…? "My old- fashioned father was a priest," he shrugged.

The hotel in Belgrade was cold: the heat would be turned on only October 15. Two weeks to go! To keep warm for the rest of the day, at breakfast men downed cognac. Even I poured a teaspoon of rum in my afternoon tea, but during the evenings of lectures and then conversations in cafes, I kept a clear head.

Yes, I lost my heart several times over.

No, I doubt Jerzy would have defected, with his wife back in Warsaw, a sort of hostage of the regime while he was abroad. He insisted Poland would liberalize, writers' unpublished "dangerous" works would see print, he'd arrange cultural exchanges, even manage an invitation for me to come as a visiting American writer.

We're having trout tonight! In Belgrade, the Serbian Writers' Union served Lake Ochrin trout. Jerzy boned it one- handed, refused help. Yes, I was conscious of his other, empty, sleeve.

Our last evening in Belgrade, everyone else headed toward cafes and meetings, enjoyed much drinking and singing. Jerzy and I slipped away to walk along the Danube. Over the fortress, the full moon doubled itself in the river, reflections sliced by the wake of a barge. I shivered: Jerzy put his jacket around me… I worried about his catching cold, his overtiring—he might have a weak heart from such a life of walking tightropes—so I treated him with deference due an elder writer. The lines on his face were like rings on cut trees, the scars knotholes…The sap still ran warm in the moon. He implied he would like to love me.

Oh—you insist—he obviously did!

No, though the night was romantic, and Jerzy accustomed to danger, he loved his wife, I loved my absent lover. And shadows came alive along the riverbank. We filed dutifully back into the hotel lobby where heavy-set men sat in overstuffed chairs pretending to read newspapers, like the bellhops and bartenders reporting for one side or another.

We sat down at a little table and ordered tea with a shot glass of rum…Two Parisian writers approached to discuss translating Jerzy's books into French. A Finn showed off his unpublished manuscript. A Belorussian with a Leica was constantly snapping photographs "for the conference scrapbook." The Rumanian's watchdog passed, half hiding "decadent" magazines, nudes on the cover…The West German journalist paused to ask for a match, and Jerzy stiffened. When the East German delegation sat down at the next table, he quickly invited me to move to the bar, and bought one plum brandy for us to share.

Do you still feel that way about Germans? The bankers here in Toronto for the international monetary conference all act like old friends: one forgets, one adapts. Jerzy didn't.

I admitted to Jerzy that though during World War Too I was a child safe in America, I was probably more aware of the news than most American kids: my father served in the American Army, European sector, while his sister trapped in Leningrad was trying to survive the Nazi's Blockade. Other relatives were in other dangerous places…

The Polish delegation—including their nyanushkas—returned from their night on the town, waved a circular wave, headed for the elevator. Jerzy walked me up the broad stairs. "Please wait—" He disappeared, returned, book in hand… Although we could not read each other's language, outside my hotel room we traded our books autographed with discreet affection. Of my own books, only one hardback was published then, plus two skinny chapbooks. We would all be heading home the next days, so I gave all the copies to Jerzy. Some libraries in Warsaw would have a shelf for foreign books, and censors would be bored by poetry

He bowed. His lips kissed my hand, his eyes kissed my lips. "Good night, child."

I did feel like a child beside him…Alone in my chilly hotel room, trying to transliterate the Polish into the Cyrillic alphabet in European alphabet which I was somewhat able to figure out, I deciphered the titles of all his publications, positions, awards, dates. Numbers betrayed: we were born the same year. I examined the mirror: his lines etched my face. Would I also lose an arm at the shoulder?

Next morning, lugging my suitcase to the communal taxi where a couple of French writers were already inside, I looked back at the hotel. Six stories over the river, with his one hand he waved, then with that one hand blew a kiss. From the street I waved back with both arms, flicked kisses in return. The cabbie honked, a Finnish writer crammed his long legs inside, and our shared taxi careened through the Belgrade traffic to the airport.

Through several security check-points, while about to queue for boarding, I looked through the glass barrier: there he stood. He set down his briefcase. Now I blew kisses back. He signaled he'd come through the checkpoints in a moment, but he was still at the ticket counter when in five languages the loudspeaker announced my flight.

Awaiting our respective take-offs, our planes side by side on the tarmac, he waved behind the sealed window of his East-bound plane, I wave from behind the sealed window of my West-bound plane.

Perhaps we would always be waving…

***

Jerzy's letters on light blue airmail paper didn't appear opened by censors…Maybe he asked some visiting tourist to mail them abroad…I didn't want to get him in trouble, he was enough of a risk-taker, so since letters with American stamps would attract too much attention, I sent my new poems via a close American friend flying to Warsaw on business, she would slip them into a Polish mailbox or even look up his office. As an "official" poet, Jerzy might even receive her at the Polish Writers Union—

In an air gram she wrote, "Between language classes I've tried to find your friend, got lost in unfamiliar sections of town. I don't believe I was followed: I'm small, my clothes deliberately shabby, unlike a tourist's. His wife—flaxen-haired, my height, cabbage cooking—whispered through a crack in the door, "He is busy, call some other day." She did not ask me in, would not give the phone number. "You will find it." Directories here are out-dated and scarce, but I found one, and a working street-corner phone. "He is on vacation," she murmured. The next week: "He is in hospital, please go away." "What's wrong with him?" "His heart—his head," the wife said. I left and from down on the street below I noticed that from her window, she watched my departure. In a doorway across the street, I spotted a man I always see on my bus and in the same restaurants. What should I do next? I'm still learning the language."

My correspondent was unaware 'hospital' was likely a euphemism for 'prison.'

Later other friends visiting Warsaw friends wrote: "Apparently your friend checked himself into a psychiatric asylum. Legitimate clinic, not one of those Soviet-style institutions. He emerged with some new manuscript, later it got published." They were unaware of title or subject.

Jerzy wrote to me once more, about a projected visit to another literary festival, but did not mention any new book.

Then my friends learned he re-entered that psychiatric asylum. Maybe he went into exile inside. Safer to play a stranger studying the territory of madness? One can forge peculiar passports at the borders of sanity. Authorities may even have believed him, as they riffled the elegant baggage he invented for the journey. Paranoia is ordinary as a dressing gown spotted with omelet. Only the elixir of candor that leaks from the improperly-screwed bottle cap of his brain could give him away.

Perhaps better he remained officially insane, you say? Safe from the turmoil and truncheons of pretenses and arrests?

Madame Somebody reminds me that they are ordering dessert, won't I yield to a chocolate mousse? And now tell us about yourself— You are some sort of aspiring American writer?

Best we wait until another time. Right now, discussions around us concern art as an investment. The other guests buy best sellers, support the opera, hang trendy paintings...But a living working artiste in their midst makes some people nervous. So you, my dear host, early switched from creation of poems to creation of wealth? Thank goodness, for this mousse is delicious, and you hold all the credit cards.

Your guests want to hear the rest of my story? I do not know the rest of the story...

We tried to learn more , friends wrote after their sojourn in Poland,

about why he jumped from that government- building window...
His book had something to do with insanity.

You offer to research, dear host? Still have connections, can check old obits? You suspect he *was suicided.*

"Defenestrated ," you call it. Possibly he had been forced to write propaganda for the regime, a standard chore there, or denunciations, inadvertently might have betrayed a friend.

Perhaps better not to know.

Though I keep searching, I cannot remember his last name... Began with K, sounded like a sneeze, but no, not Kosinski...Nothing on the Internet about a one-armed Polish novelist. Nor have I found his book on my burgeoning shelves. His letters are in some stored carton.

"Then what is the point of your story?" Madame Somebody in-quires.

"Seems inconclusive," another dinner guest murmurs. "Frankly, pointless..."

Mmmm...Could that be the whole point...Do you need me to wrap up the story with a tidy bow? If I cannot give you a real-hot-romance, should we shrug this off as one more stranger-on-a-train encounter, *grand amour manqué ,* a could-be lover who disappears from orbit, leaves no return address...

Thanks, no coffee, tonight I must sleep. Thank you for the ele-gant supper...

Next time, yes, I could tell you a different story...if no more con-clusive finale. Could that be the point? So I could not give you a real-hot-romance. Should we therefore shrug this off as another stranger-on-a-train encounter, *grand amour manqué,* a could-be lover who disappears from orbit, leaves no return address...

Next time, I could tell different tales from the conference, if with no more conclusive finales...The Rumanian poet—My old love from Dalmatia. another who waited in the wings until—Thank you for such an elegant supper!

His surname? His surname...I wrote an acquaintance named

Kamila whose origin is Polish. She searched the Internet and emailed me:

I enjoyed your s tory online, it made me think about whatever writers I know named Jerzy. Looks like you met Jerzy Krzyszton. I was a kid when my parents got his book "Obled"— means Insanity. I was too young then to read i t then, but did years later. I am pretty sure he i s the one- armed-Pole f rom your story... He lost his arm when he was a kid...

No need, dear host, to mention that many over there disappear, or *are disappeared*, leave no trace…

Jerzy left a legacy.

Lookout
Material: Bronze
Size: 4H x 4W x 12L

Day Sailor
Material: Bronze
Size: 6H x 10W

Maybe It Was the Moths

INNOCENT FLOUR MOTHS that don't bite, merely breed and multiply in kitchens, escape capture with deft aerial acrobatics, hover at the perimeter of vision, claim every box of crackers, cookies, pasta box as home. Flour moths that mate, exponentially multiply, rule what's human territory. *His* territory.

Flour moths were driving them, at least him, nuts. Mattie, claiming hitherto-unknown entomological interests, called them "fluttering shadows of dark angels…And flour moths don't sting, honey, and they vanish in a puff of wing-flakes, powdery dust…"

"Dark specks on the white linoleum counter, smudge on the white fridge," he countered.

When one moth landed in her iced coffee, though she refused to call exterminators, at least she weighed the idea of moth-flakes as long as they were organic, and admitted those bags of bread-flour and sugar must be transferred to sealable jars.

She must transfer, active form of the verb or was it a pronoun, those bags of bread-flour and sugar, period.

Rescue me—

Maybe July's heat was making him as jumpy as those crickets in his home office in the cellar. At least in his cellar, he could insert his favorite Country Western CDs into his computer. He would download more someday if he had the patience.

Mattie was impatient with his impatience. People got impatient in drought. All week they'd needed a good storm to water the garden and cool things off. One cloud hung limp overhead but the sky held.

Maybe it was the itching. How poison ivy rashes persist! He needed more and stronger calamine lotion quickly!

Rescue me

Come on and take—

Maybe it was because tonight's guest-of-honor had just last week

53

been appointed an ambassador of sorts, surely thanks to generous campaign contributions in his wife's maiden name, a lady reputed independently wealthy. The country to which the suddenly-Honorable was being posted, his first, was small, hot and restive, otherwise relatively uninteresting. Like the guest- of-honor himself. An oilman, the Honorable called the posting abroad "higher calling, adding a spattering of history and geography to my geology." Now at least the Honorable might become somewhat more interesting.

Rescue me

Come on and take my heart —

Even before he could adjust his computer, the lyrics kept playing through his head.

"Honey, the silver's tarnished!"

Mattie insisted on polishing the silver again. Even pieces not intended for use tonight. "But what if unexpectedly the ambassador's wife wants tea? Can't pretend that tarnished pot is ancestral pewter."

Mattie sent Henry for silver polish: she must continue making cinnamon meringues and this required concentration. He proudly bought home quick-fix anti-tarnish liquid.

"But honey, this is not the paste! Real paste polish may take more rubbing but lasts longer! With the cheapo stuff, our wedding silver could disintegrate!"

He'd at least remembered to buy organic moth-flakes, which he scattered but she swept up.

Maybe he was—*testy* —because despite his requests, she still called him "honey."

Rescue me

Come on and take my heart

Take your love and conquer every part—

Maybe because mostly what he received on his computer these days—in addition to the intriguing emails to his second, covert, address—was SPAM advertising Viagra and Cialis. He'd suspect Mattie of tactfully having it sent it to him but 1) she barely knew how to open a computer and 2) didn't seem to care much about that aspect of marriage. Mattie claimed "no time for fancy dye jobs." Her hair was mouse-color, moth-color.

What she wore was what she wore, no time to shop. Tonight, though, it'd be some new thing he'd see later.

The ambassador's wife, upon one distant sighting since college, remained slender and elegant, obsidian satin hair sliding long over tanned shoulders.

He added a line to the email he was surreptitiously tapping on his other account, confirming where he was to meet the artist whose nude self-portraits flashed on the web.

Take your love
and conquer every part—

As if joined by telepathy, the mysterious painter-lady was spinning that same song. He'd emailed her to learn if she knew who Fontella Bass was, or was it *were* , and the lady answered that she listened to that song on her own car radio too but that her husband couldn't stand that brand of music. Henry answered that he suffered similar spousal challenges. Mattie's tastes were Vivaldi and Bach, played and replayed on the old 33-&-1/3s passed down from her cousin Clarinda. He liked them too, but not constantly.

Rescue me
'Cause I'm lonely
And I'm blue

He'd wear his blue polo shirt for their first rendezvous. The appliquéd alligator was frayed at the tail but this might reach the lady's heart. And the big blue jaws hinted at his— amorous avarice. Most of her nudes were painted hues of blue. The tryst, if he could call it that, yet, would be just an innocent glass of wine or iced tea when they ran into each other as if by chance in the mall two towns over.

Now, in his raggedly grey tee, trying not to hum those darn lyrics, he went upstairs and prowled the kitchen. It didn't help Mattie's mood that, though he complimented her on her culinary skills, he stuck a finger in her shimmering aspic, next into a powered doughy things, and then into her impeccably decorated mango sherbets. This taste-testing habit from his first childhood would prepare for his second, which, she remarked, would not be far away.

This existence is all so banal, back at his computer he tapped out. *Couldn't we liven it up somehow? 'Cause I'm lonely*

And I'm blue

Rescue me—

The cellar door opened, and he signed off. It didn't help that Mattie interrupted him in the midst of scratching while ostensibly figuring how to adapt his complex layouts for A Small American Suburban Town for possible use in the future ambassador's host country; might they invite him over to help implement them?

C'mon over and rescue us—

Mattie wondered how, given his inferior math skills, any of his buildings and bridges stood upright. She was a substitute arithmetic teacher who handled their own taxes, by hand since she claimed "Computers hurt the eyes."

His structures not only stood firm, (or should it be firmly?) but their creation monetarily supported them both.

Mattie interrupted him twice to ask if he'd remembered ice while buying tonight's wine but where was it? "And I haven't seen any extra cubes in the freezer compartment. I thought you'd made more ice, or bought a bag—still in the car in this hot weather? Didn't you remember to take the cooler?

Shouldn't you be cooling the white wine, opening the red to let it breathe?"

In truth, he'd not visited the liquor store yet. Besides, he himself could not drink anymore since taking those new pills, which also undermined his—was it "libido?"

Come and rescue me

Take me in your arms

The lady's paintings weren't porn, they were classy, artsy, but the muscles on the arms and butts were particularly sensuous. As for the breasts—

"Between the moths and the deer—" Henry mumbled as he tested a pot c on the stove.

Yes, the blasted deer. It didn't help that the small swimming pool installed in their yard wasn't yet fenced. Driven from their woods by new housing developments, deer considered this garden a refuge for threatened wildlife, and pruned the plantings. Yesterday an inquisitive yearling invaded the garden. Alas, if this was his pseudo castle, it looked like every other saltbox on the block.

Tree frogs and bullfrogs, which Maggie considered "particularly lovely at dusk, with their chirps and basso harrumphs," also invaded the pool. Neither ribets nor deer minded chlorine. Hadn't he poured enough?

Nor did it help that last November, Canada geese landed in the nearby golf course, refused to re-migrate this July, fertilized the golf course with souvenir cigars, and settled around his swimming pool. As if the deer didn't do enough.

Their neighbor Bud, a retired colonel, scared critters from his yard with target-practice, and offered Mattie, "a New Year's goose for first course before the freshly-killed venison we're gonna roast in the yard." She shuddered, answered she would leave the game for his wife, Darletta.

Darletta, of the nasal whine and lack of *gs* on her gerunds: *Everythin' was talkin', walkin', goin'*

Darletta was small, extremely blonde, and always callin' Henry over to excise somethin', always requirin' assistance—

Rescue me

This morning while Mattie was stirring aspic and spinning old Vivaldis, and he was wondering how en route to the liquor store he might vanish for ten minutes to practice his drives on the golf course and use the phone-box. Online, the painter lady's voice had been swan's down as she toyed with his idea of a face-to-face meeting two towns over tomorrow—he deserved a break from his drawing board and domesticity.

Meanwhile a swan had settled on Darletta-and-Bud's-Koi- Pond. A fancy wrought-iron sign announced their ownership, but as Bud had complained to Mattie, the darn swans were illiterate.

Now Darletta was hysterical on the phone. "Bud's off somewhere shootin' something', and there's a goose or swan—so couldn't you, Henry darlin', come over—"

This time Mattie insisted on going next door: "Henry is finishing his urban-planning project. And he is uneasy with wildlife. I'm the bird-watcher."

Mattie watched everything. About watching snakes, though, she was flat-out phobic, "flat-out" not inappropriate: upon discovering the six-foot black rat-catcher raiding nests in their garden, then slithering through their open kitchen door, she fainted flat-out, something girls like Mattie who major in civil engineering weren't supposed to do.

Everyone had predicted that marriage to Henry, in commercial architecture, would be a good partnership—of course it was—though she'd not managed to engineer a computer or much more than the early childhood learning of a few schoolchildren, and thank goodness, doing the taxes.

Henry had been riffed from the big downtown architectural office to a home office where, as Maggie put it, "undistracted by traditional office distractions, you can peacefully telecommute."

"Henry darlin', please come over and save me!"

This invasive swan turned out to be a huge stallion of a male, who hunched his feathers twice his original size. Zeus Incarnate, the creature clambered up the bank of Darletta-and- Bud's Koi-Pond with powerful waddles and hisses—weren't these supposed to be mute swans?

Mattie glimpsed through the reeds on the far side a smaller swan with four gray-brown cygnets. She was thrilled. Darletta was not.

"Help, rescue me! Somebody quickly—"

The male marched closer and closer, frightening the ladies. Mattie retreated with Darletta to their lanai or whatever those sterile glassed-in patios were called, and Bud lumbered in to recall how raccoons also menaced the koi but he'd set a spring trap. Now he could again set the trap, capture the bird, and cook up swan stew. Horrified, Mattie remarked her cauldron was surely over boiling, there'd be tomato aspic all over her kitchen, and she fled to recount the recounting to Henry.

Mattie felt guilty these next-yard neighbors weren't on tonight's guest list not only because they lacked ties to the ambassadorial world, but Henry frankly couldn't abide Bud. "Numerous people you can't abide," Mattie noted.

They had set the table for eight—now down to six because this morning one couple phoned with an out-of-town funeral.

Why couldn't people schedule their funerals at times more convenient to the living?

Six other old college classmates had accepted tonight's celebratory dinner with the newly-appointed ambassador, already in the throes of moving, the wife overseeing the "packing in this heat." American air conditioning was not guaranteed to function without interruption in their forthcoming post, and as if deliberately to give the Honorables a draught of reality, today brought brownouts in their own safe American neighborhood.

Henry was already perspiring. Another reason for what Mattie labeled his bad-temper. He didn't mean to snarl, he truly didn't. The more he snarled, the more dulcet her tones: he knew this was how she was trained to control a fractious classroom.

Come on baby and rescue me

Didn't help either that his project, over which he was laboring, was seeking new clients abroad because their local suburban planning commission, initially interested, had been enticed by another company which bid a few thousand less.

Then due to the legal wrangling, last Friday the aged owner of the adjoining property–his mini-golf course— announced donation of her land to a sect which believed in— Heaven knew what. Surveyors' teams had arrived with tripods and telescopes, and the greens were already being torn up for a cemetery! Bulldozers must have been waiting for grave action and the legal stuff was merely pro forma…

So, even enjoying his own puns, he was not in the best of humor. "You seldom are," Mattie said, "though I bend over backward to humor you."

Didn't help that Henry expected her to set the bumpy rosebuds-and-daisies china inherited from his Great Aunt Edna in Elmira via his cousin Grace, whom Mattie never particularly enjoyed, "and that pattern is really passé." She preferred her old roommate's hand-thrown pottery, every piece slightly different, frankly seconds. "This way the Honorables would not be upstaged," she said, "in case their own china is not up to diplomatic status."

Henry's plates bumpy as toads, teacups eggshell fragile he himself might have labeled "old-fashioned lower middle class rural Sunday-best" if these hadn't been his side of the family, but she—he—*should* use this china set tonight.

Relatives also expected Henry and Mattie to increase the over-population rate. Yet copulation didn't seem to matter much to Mattie, an admitted neatness-freak, who may have found the messiness of that activity distasteful.

Finally Mattie set ten places with his rosebud legacy. "Ten is too many!"

"You never know who, at the last minute—"

The fact that the latest of Mattie's perennial diets made her, frankly, cranky, didn't help either. She may have intimated—she could be so subtle he often couldn't decipher what she meant—it was the lack of romantic activity these nights, but he couldn't help that. Yet an encounter with that painter lady—

Rescue me

Take me in your arms
I want your tender charms

Yes, a banal rhyme, if indeed he had it right. That charming lady at the other end of their email correspondence had written that she herself was "not like my buxom nudes." He'd found her website self-portraits "sinewy, slim, and succulent."

He'd been supposedly ordering chlorine in bulk online but Googled wrong and landed on the lady artist's link, and kept that link handy.

Mattie, looking over his shoulder the first time—weeks ago—he happened on the knock-out website, called them "anorexic porn pix."

"Honey! Shouldn't we uncork the merlot so it has time to breathe?" she asked now. "The first dinner guests could arrive at any moment!"

One couple inevitably turned up early, as if deliberately to catch the hosts with their slips and chips, straps and patches, showing.

Rescue me

Where in hell were his khaki shorts? He'd left them drying over the shower rail. Claiming that Henry has not really washed them clean enough, Mattie had swiped them for the washing machine! Granted he never got them clean as the machine, why would she choose to wash laundry this day! And hang it out on the line—dryer-fixer-man coming Monday—though she worried that hanging out clothes would make it rain. Please, not tonight. And she argued that Henry was challenging her simplest statement.

"Look out the window!" he answered. "We might get rain after all. And please don't call me 'honey' in front of guests."

"If I said the sky was blue you'd point out clouds!"

He didn't challenge whether she should have used "were" instead of "was;" he'd become unsure of his conditionals or were they subjunctives? Many people nowadays seemed unaware grammar existed.

He buttoned his white shirt and zipped gray wool trousers though he yearned for shorts on his poison-ivied legs. Drought hadn't killed that shiny patch of poison ivy. Deer reputedly relished it, though what had become *their* deer did not.

Calamine pinked his rashes and now decided him to postpone the long-desired encounter with the lady. He flashed another email, *Sorry, I am indisposed, l e t 's schedule rescue operations for next week—*

He tried to skip a necktie tonight but Mattie insisted. His old moccasins must pass: this was, after all, also his home, and moccasins were easier on the itches. To hell with two-bit ambassadors, anyway, though this ambassador had been a classmate. Henry had glimpsed the nascent ambassador's future wife way across the campus.

Mattie appeared in a new greenish orange dress, which she called "a mottled orangey-avocado muumuu." The loose sack hid more obvious flaws. She had flaws these days. "Honey, how does—what do you think the ambassador's wife will—"

Out the window he watched a breeze disturb the surface of the pool, sending patterns of reflections climbing the pine, ripples racing up the trunk, into branches like real water, like shadows. Whitish shadows—

The stallion swan settled into their swimming pool, followed by his lady swan with four moth-brown cygnets. Must go chase the damn things—

In passing he popped one of Mattie's hot meringues into his mouth, then another. Distracted yet again, again they went over the seating arrangement and tonight's menu. But Mattie interrupted: "You forgot to buy shrimps! Run out to the seafood trucks stand to buy six pounds!"

The "stand" was only the back of a pickup from South Carolina, but their shrimps were fresh and the truck parked only a couple of blocks away in their "neighborhood." Mattie said she wouldn't have time to shell, so he must.

He forgot the wine again but maybe someone would bring a jug. Finally he found the corkscrew, an item which should always be handy—A jug would have a screw top.

He worried Mattie would bring up drilling in the Arctic, old classmates would argue Red Sox versus Yankees versus their memories of their own college team, certain democrats would set flames blazing from the ears of certain republicans. The Honorables must have contributed to the recent campaigns—

"Since that last-minute funeral in New Jersey knocked one couple off the list, maybe we should've invited Darletta and Bud to fill out the table, they must've noted all our activity…"

Henry persuaded Mattie to phone and pretend he'd thought Mattie had invited them and she'd thought he had, so even though it was so late would they, she'd already set their two places—

As he shelled the shrimps, he remembered the email lady once mentioned being allergic to shellfish, and now he worried the ambassador's wife might be also. She could even be vegetarian. Chunks of beef were marinating in the last inches of their screw-top jug burgundy. The beef Mattie had bought in the guests' honor: "They mightn't have much fresh meat in that Third-World country."

"Rice?"

"Moths in it so I scattered it for the birds."

"But dry rice can puff up in their little bird stomachs!" "Lettuce from the garden?"

"If the deer—"

Mattie promised to do the shopping herself next time, she'd find various organic sprays against moths and poison ivy and deer. "Tomorrow. But if you're right it'll rain, wash all that poison into the pool—Our swans—yes, ours now—Did you remember, honey, to get—Oh, those dark clouds filling the blue spaces in the sky! Maybe we are living in different spaces nowadays."

True…If he were younger, he—He sometimes speculated.

Rescue me

Need me, baby

Guests were arriving. Two-by-two, as if creatures into Noah's Ark, which the house was about to become: the thunderstorm broke, the pool was overflowing, lawn and cellar might flood, critters might already be seeking shelter in their cellar and attic—

Bud wore not a jacket and tie like the other male guests but his usual Red-Sox tee. Darletta appeared in a shiny purple something V-necked almost to her waist. Henry pictured the ambassador's wife in tight black, similarly cleavaged.

Guests blessedly brought good white wine, and French champagne, chilled, in the future ambassador's honor, instead of the usual jug of California red. The future ambassador inquired whether he could have a scotch instead.

Bud said he had scotch next door, he'd get it, and surely someone would prefer beer? He did. "We gotta a case of Boars Head in our basement. No, don't worry, I don't mind rain, I gotta to change into a dress shirt anyway—"

All found plenty to drink while the guests-of-honor were dishonorably late, and later. *Time like a determined swan ...* Was he only quoting himself, or the email from the lady, or Mattie?

Surely it was his own original thought, though of late Mattie accused him of seldom entertaining original thoughts. Not so, damn it!

As background music, Mattie put on *The Seasons* for the third and scratchiest time. *Spring* turned into *Winter*, *Winter* to—

The guests decimated the canapés and were rapidly draining the wine.

"I heard somewhere, I think at the War College where I spent a month," Bud was saying, though it was Henry who'd told Mattie who must have told Darletta, "that General MacArthur even as a colonel always arrived late for dinners. At the last-minute, the other guests hungry but needing to wait on protocol, the general's aide would fling open the host's door,

MacArthur would fling his cape off his shoulders for the aide to gather up—"

"*Cape!* For Pete's sake!"

"Maybe your high-falutin ambassadors are looking for their rain capes this tropical night—"

It was ever later and wetter, the canapés crumbling, the level of wine ever lower, indeed disappearing. Henry opened the last box of crackers. Three moths flew out. Everyone politely inspected Henry's office and drawing board, tested and screwed up his new computer. Bud noticed that the storm was leaking into Henry's basement, Mattie brought up Arctic drilling, democrats and republicans were waving red flags, three flour moths graced the marinade, and everyone hinted they might like to sit down.

"We'd better phone them, honey. You."

He dialed. "No answer. They must be on their way." Darletta bumped the turntable and the records shattered.

Bud picked up a saucer and dropped it.

"My old language lady instructor at Monterey," Bud said, "claimed breaking saucers brings luck. It didn't bring me luck on my exams, but why not break those old records and test whether—?"

"You've got those Indian Mealy Moths tooooo!" Darletta slurred as one landed in her wine. "But we got real good pesticide!"

Mattie looked horrified.

"The Agent Orange of bug-killers. I'll get it—" Bud wove home again through the puddles. He returned with another six- pack of beer instead. "Guess I used up all the Pesticide on the yard last week…The rain's stopped, pools overflowing, but I scared the swans, they're gone for the night."

Swan scat on his shoes marked the white rug.

The guests around the table were all but banging their cutlery on the elegant plates. The Honorables might or might not turn up sometime but the guests would be unwieldy if they didn't eat…

They left no leftovers, though Mattie noticed two untouched jumbo shrimp that had escaped the pot and put them into the refrigerator for the morrow…

* * *

After the guests departed, Mattie reiterated that she'd never excuse those Honorables for having gone somewhere else.

They cleaned up till two. Mattie swept up the shattered rosebuds-and-daisies and black-wax shards, never mind who was responsible. Might the shattered saucer indeed bring luck? Henry's—libido—felt strangely liberated and he was sure his blood pressure had dropped by half despite the ambassadorial pair standing them up. As the cellar was already half flooded, half asleep he unplugged his computer and lugged it upstairs to the dining room and plugged it in.

Mattie stripped off her hot muumuu. Down to her lace slip, her hair tousled, she was, he decided, surprisingly fetching. At two a.m., he ordered online two last-minute cheap- fare flights to Iceland three days hence. "Why not add the Arctic?" Mattie asked. "Couldn't it be almost warm in July?"

He did. No damned critters there except—oh, yes, polar bears. Though Mattie might try to feed them Oreos, with luck they'd keep to themselves. He also discovered, at 2:30 a.m., that Mattie was not, after all, adverse to athletic nocturnal activity.

Neither, to his further surprise, in the morning either.

The following noon, that somewhere the future ambassador had been turned out to be a Soho gallery opening of the wife's oils—they hadn't even known she dabbled in painting—but how could anyone have mixed up the dates?

"You may be the forgiving sort, honey," Mattie argued, "but no matter how important an ambassador is supposed to be, an ambassador's wife should have manners as well as an engagement calendar!"

He took the two leftover giant shrimps to Darletta and Bud. Meanwhile Mattie packed her clothes and those of his she felt he should wear in Reykjavik and in the Arctic—"No, honey, we won't pack your old baseball shirts or Hawaiian-patterned shorts…Best throw the leftover popover to the swans, they don't like the crumbs of my cinnamon meringues—"

Maybe the flour moths would.

Little Mermaid
Material: Pink Alabaster
Size: 12H x 10W x 14L

Beyond Laramie

SNOW IS A RAGGED WINDING SHEET crumpled in the hollows on the northeast slopes. Sun and wind shear snow off most of the sandstone boulders, wind smoothes their edges, they blend with the beige grasses and low brush. Snow clings to fingers on the hillsides, split open like a cake or corpse, show striations of ivory and gray, maroon and black. Bone and sinew, are all I can think, and blood and char.

The terrible, magnificent, blue of the sky is relieved by two shabby clouds over this land of space and slice and slide. The few slashes of black are stark against the sere background and foreground: tatters of a plastic bag caught on a fence, one black horse near an isolated shed, black skeletons of trees.

Near-black are the triangles of conifers planted in rare rows to hold back snow. Obsidian the jagged chunks, like creature frozen to statues while dancing, discus throwing, or dying.

Obsidian my hair, obsidian my eyes.

All else is the shade of a dirty camel who dumps his dung across deserts. Camel, my color. I am the international refugee from a country barely on the map, an undocumented immigrant of undetermined age or sex, a universal donor with no more blood to give.

Cold is inimical to this body, this soul, which tries to recall—and the soul can recall, memory is not the dominion only of the mind—the humid warmth of equatorial lands, their shouts, shootings, dangerous cacophonies. And laughter. Here, a laugh is but a howl of wind, the yowl of a coyote who bemoans the fled antelopes. Danger is not frozen out, menaces are only congealed, waiting.

What good is nostalgia? How can a marked man return to lands torn apart, yet still bound in ancient arguments? Each group is steeped in the rivalries of generations—generations not beyond recall, for within each clan or cluster, elders keep the rivalries alive, burnish and pass on their ferocious quarrels.

In this barren winter landscape, can there be enough inhabitants to stoke old feuds? People move away to pleasant places, or die on the hills and in the depressions between hills. A few quarrels are re-membered, the way records of births and deaths are maintained by unknown archivists whose work is of scant interest either to visitors or even to the sparse settlers.

Freight trains, sealed gray rectangles containing unknown cargo, snake like well-fed pythons across the horizon. Express trucks speed the mail but who would write to me? On far highways, huge noisy rectangles of double-trucks transport food and goods, but who is there to buy? All these damn desert flies? *I* am here, but don't dare appear.

On the outskirts of isolated towns, between shuttered industrial sites and residential streets where lights are extinguished by nine o'clock, used-car lot workers hose vehicles clean of dust. Street lights reflect wild eyes on the hoods and roofs until the night's dust dims them again.

Vehicles are securely locked: not a one where I might crawl in and sleep a few warm hours until just before dawn. At dawn I would move on before the sun brought people out.

En route I will pause at a truck stop where nobody asks questions or tries to make friends. Were I to speak one word, polite and quick: my accent would betray. But truck stops are miniature oases with good trash bins...

Mine was a jumble of accents in countries steeped in heat and the glistening green of enormous leaves shot through with veins and stripes of dark-greens and light-greens, leaves blood- speckled green, their stripes and pistils crimson, in jungles swarming with frogs, mon-keys, insects, birds and serpents in rainbows of color. Everyone, every-thing, wet with rain or mist, waterfall or flood. The smell of bloom, decay, rebirth, re-bloom. Deserts smell of sand and smoke, dust and mysteries.

Here, cold freezes secrets: only later the secrets may thaw and dissolve in space. Seeming freedom frightens and liberates. Over every land, the moon, full or slivered, on occasion reveals secrets below but mostly hides them.

I carry my back-story as if in my knapsack, buckled shut.

Others can only guess at its contents from bulges, from clues that leak out. I pull a guillotine on my past, my future, a story that could have happened beyond The End, but maybe did not.

For even out here, though one can elude them for a while, the shadowers, the watchers, remain alert as pit bulls, or as those coyotes howling beyond the next hill. A lone hawk and an unsubstantial clutter of blackbirds monitor my progress.

As in chess, where a few pieces still stand but are stymied, and no longer shadow across unoccupied squares, any move I weigh is dangerous. Go forward, backwards, dogleg or diagonally? Satisfactory resolution is elusive.

No need to make a statement, notify, help or hurt another individual, concern myself with immortality. No desire to trail or trace riddles, guessing games regarding nationality or age, gender or blood type. Others can think whatever they want, imagine what went before. Few of their conjectures would be correct. None matter. I need only locate the simplest path across the hills into a slim crevasse. I have no regrets, rather a sense of a final chapter written, my destiny fulfilled.

Hosiah and Mike and Sukie with Her Damned Melon

LAMB CHOPS in burgundy, oysters in white wine, my goats, rum home rum— Lamb chops, oysters, my goats, my goats, rum home rum—damn the gunshots— damn the med shots—Home rum home—My neg-lected goats—

The chant resounded in Hosiah's head even while Nurse Annie insisted on taking surgical scissors to his tangled hair: "because, sweetie, your outdated hippie braid and squirrels'- nest beard sponge up dribbles."

Now, beardless and with almost a crew cut and surely unrecognizable, he had visitors. Sukie's guy, after gashing his biceps on a barn beam he was raising, brought the girl along to the hospital's EMERGENCY, where Doc Scoples approximated and stitched together the edges of his ripped dragon tattoos, then invited them to follow him to the ward where he must check Hosiah's injuries and listen to his heart. "Captain Ho there beat me swimming from his dad's marina to the lighthouse when we were eight, and now he's running the marina and I'm a doctor checking his injuries. What the—"

Sukie, clutching her Raggedy Andy, was drinking the "milkshakes" from every bed-tray in the ward, disconnecting and reconnecting blinking machines if not always to the same tubes. Nurse Annie ran after her and brought her into the room.

"Captain Ho!" Sukie said. "Your hair used to be rusty like Mutt's, now you've all white like Uncle Mike! Where's your beard?" Then, lifting her smock, she went on: "Wanna see my watermelon? Growing bigger! Father's real mad."

Doc Scoples turned his stethoscope to Sukie's belly, then told Hosiah, "Tell her parents—"

"Can't tell her parents anything, Doc," Hosiah said.

Couldn't say goddamned parents around Nurse Annie. "They

71

threw her out when she began to swell up. She's staying in my cabin, that's the old Marina office."

"With you here in hospital, and your Marianne away, who is keeping an eye on her?"

"Marianne, who was super-educated, claimed she hadn't been trained to deal with 'challenged' children. Waldo Green, my partner who lives across the marina, and Edna in the doublewide up the hill, they see that Sukie fixes her peanut butter-and-jelly sandwich and makes the school bus. The driver knows to deliver her to the building with the parenting classes. After school, her guy picks her up and delivers her back to my marina. Not on his Harley anymore, she's too big now…When they imprisoned me in this damned hospital, Mutt apparently dug a hole under the cabin and mostly stays there, barely eats. Sukie lured him out with the kibbles for the goats. But me stuck here, I worry about the girl, and my goats, and Mutt, and my cats… The girl—"

"I live a block away from here," Nurse Annie said. "Got a spare room, could board her, but not your critters, till time."

"When's time?" Hosiah wondered. "When'll I be outta here? When can I get back to drinking real drinks?" Nurses ground pills into applesauce, discussed the elderly loss of smell. Nonsense, though not a bad thing as hospital smells nasty. He missed goat milk, a damn sight healthier than Ensure or those pureed green beans, and he downright craved that sea-glass flask of rum.

Sukie reached into her Mickey Mouse backpack, and pulled out a pear. He could smell this pear was ripe, fragrant—

"No fruit, Ho," from the doorway Doc interrupted. "Nothing from sea, land or air."

Sukie herself nibbled the pear. "Salty…" Then, Doc gone and Nurse Annie making another bed farther up the ward, she held it out to Hosiah. He hesitated, then grabbed and bit.

Slightly briny as the pear tree roots soaked up storm tides, but, delicious! Hosiah finished it as a policeman entered.

"Excuse me, sir, need information about the shooting accident."

"No accident, officer," Hosiah said. "Someone shot me on purpose...Hey, weren't you the Benton's kid, Tommy, crabbing off my Marina? And 'borrowing' my cokes?"

"Captain Hosiah! Years ago...And I fell off riding your billy goat...Okay, just a minute, I'll get you another coke from the machine down the hall—" He vanished, and two minutes later reappeared, snapping open the tab.

"Thanks, Tommy." Hosiah sipped it, though he would have preferred a can of beer.

"Now, sir, about the...shooting?"

"Like this..." Hosiah was nonplussed by all the "sirs,"

odd to hear in Mudville. How aptly Marianne his ex had labeled the old town, where they were still waiting for basic repairs to the causeway but the ground wasn't stable enough...Now everyone said "Mudville Cinema, Mudville Five-'n'-Dime, Mudville Purple Turtle." Turtle was where he'd met Marianne, and where they drank wedding champagne a month later.

Champagne was, however, sissy stuff, compared with rum.

When could he finally get at his flask...

He quickly resumed his account. "Okay, like this: end of season, Waldo and I haul peoples' yachts into the shipyard barn—Working boats like my MARIANNE, they stay afloat all winter—I'm repairing that antique brigantine for the museum, sanding sterncastle, caulking quarterdeck. Them museum folk want old-fashioned tools, so work's slow...I shimmy up the foremast. Next scaffold over, Waldo's scraping Mike's old oyster boat EDNA MAE, getting her ready to sell. Sukie, big as a spinnaker, waddles into the boatyard shouting, 'Womb-Doc's machine says I'm getting a baby! A boy!'

"No idea where Sukie got 'womb-doc'—Hardly knows what a womb is. I remember trying to explain about birds-and- bees, the example being my pregnant goat—Nanny's the great- great-granddaughter of that pregnant nanny Mike and I, just home from Nam and putting away beers at the fair, we plunked down cash for. By time we sobered up, the nanny'd chewed our wallets, the farmer'd disappeared...Sukie's now plump as my nanny goat—Isn't that what Marianne, my ex-, would call something like a meta-smile? Anyway, up the foremast I'm thinking, that girl's maybe slow, but it's true what they say about pregnant women—no, not myself made any pregnant— they're downright beautiful."

The officer studied Sukie singing lullabies to her doll.

"Even big-bellied, the girl is pretty and she can carry a tune..." He checked his watch. Sukie's guy checked his.

Nurse Annie scribbled her address for Sukie's guy. The officer resumed his inquiry: "About the accident, sir—".

"No accident! Bullet from somewhere deliberately hits here. Waldo sees the damned vehicle zoom away but too fast to get the license number. I fall on that busty-mermaid bowsprit, she rips my stomach. I'm sprawled in the sand, under caulking cans. Brig's loose dinghy slips off, falls, crushes my right leg.

Sukie's crying my trousers are bloody—'Does bleeding there happen to men too? Or have you died?' Waldo yanks off the dinghy offa me, runs in the marina office, dials and redials 911. Busy...Always busy. He revs up my pickup, lifts me onto the flatbed." He didn't mention that Waldo's license was suspended: too many old DUIs.

"Waldo speeds us to Mudville, Sukie's crying in the cab, me, I'm spread flat out astern, Mutt's chasing after till Waldo brakes at the light, Mutt jumps aboard. ER nurses said I shoulda waited for the ambulance—'Laid out on a grubby truck, that mongrel licking your—Crazy.' 'Cheaper'n ambulances,' I answered.

"From ER to MRI, they inject something burning, must be acid, between my hand bones, slide me into a machine like a lighted coffin, supposedly photographing inside me, jackhammers pounding worse than shrapnel in Nam. One deep bang to the right ear, high screeches on the left, or was it inside my skull, screech pop bang, and you're not allowed to twitch.

Marianne once showed me a painting of sinners-in-Hades, jolly little devils,' she called them, 'but what Hell must be.' Painter's name something like Harry Bosh. Anyway, I sure know what hell's like."

"No idea who shot you?"

"Waldo saw only—what's last over a fence. Hard to remember anything in this damned place."

"Gotta get back on the road soon but I could check in with you when you get home. Would you remember better, sir, at home—You will be going home?"

"Home! Real food, real booze!"

Nurse Annie reappeared, scowled at the half-empty coke can but the officer quickly picked it up, draining what was left himself before answering his buzzing cell phone. Hosiah chuckled inwardly at his—was it subversion? collusion? collision? whatever–of the police department. Marianne, or Mike in the old days, would have a word for this. Anyway, one of Mudville's officers-of-the-so-called-law blessedly was covering up certain misdemeanors and creating others.

"Sorry, Captain Hosiah, got a call to head to a crash— Headquarters will bring forms for you to fill out—"

"Captain Hosiah," Nurse Annie scolded as she took the crushed Coke can to put in RECYCLE. "Doc says only Ensure. We'll send a supply home with you. To wash down your meds. What keeps astronauts and old folks alive."

Astronauts' gull-shit in a can—my omnivorous goats'll drink it. Frickin' meds, the blood of the lamb gonna wash them away! He'd save that for Mike, later, over lamb chops. When Edna had phoned him at the hospital to ask how he was doing, his main worry was whether Waldo and Sukie were feeding his goats right, currying them daily and washing the nanny's udders. "I'll get chops, Ho, to welcome you home," Edna had promised. "And don't fret about no goats…"

"Lay down for me, sweetie—" Nurse Annie was saying.

You care, honey, whether for you, or for me? If you'd choose to lay or lie with me, damn it, I couldn't do much anymore…Marianne corrected people who said "lay" instead of "lie" or was it the other way around? Which was correct when? And how long before he'd lie or lay in the grave or in his own bed in the old bootlegger's house?

Too many stairs there. Better his Marina office-turned- cabin, with its low bunk, galley and head all three salvaged from wrecks, table made from a floated-in door laid atop sawhorses. Hosiah had connected the plumbing to the county's pipes, Waldo built a ramp for Mike's wheelchair, and with Mike watching from his corner, they painted walls blue, green or white from the boatyard's leftover gallons. The door gleamed red with anti-barnacle bottom paint. Sukie finger-painted imperfect fantastic animals on the wet surfaces, then on herself.

***

Hosiah was home. Mutt wagged non-stop, stretched across the cast on his master's left foot, and studied the lamb chops on the filet knife. Soaked in garlic, rosemary, stashed burgundy, these would be the tastiest chops in the life of any dog, or man…

The lamb chops not what he'd normally eat…Hosiah's life had been that of landing stripers and snappers, crabs and oysters, selling the catch to CRAB SHACK across the Marina, or too the seafood truck for Mudville's markets. Hosiah himself had mostly eaten tinned sardines on Wonder Bread from Mom- 'n'-Pop's uphill, or when people paid for his MARIANNE to take them fishing, they brought picnic baskets and left food as well as beer and bait he could use himself. The gourmet garbage fattened his goats…

Hosiah had eaten goat only when some foolish billy, nanny or kid escaped the pen, got hit on the road like a deer or raccoon, which meant venison for dinner, but usually he'd give it away. He disliked putting injured critters "out of their misery," but then was quick and sure. He'd cut himself enough repairing boats, cleaning fish, fighting wars, so wasn't freaked out by blood. He'd lay a fire in the pit, rig the spit, invite Mike and Edna from their doublewide, Waldo from beyond the boatyard, even Sukie, that skinny girl who lacked all her marbles and hung around Hosiah's Marina.

"Her preacher-parents still say your marina's full of low life," Edna said.

"Not low!" Hosiah wheeled his decrepit chair closer to Mike's. "They should come down here, see for themselves."

"They call you....a dirty... old... boozer,'" Mike stammered. "Low-lifes... they claim...are in the marina—"

Marianne his ex had chided Hosiah for not looking at his listeners when on his non-stop talking jags, but too hard to look at Mike's half-paralyzed face, eternally glum.

"Sukie's parents bottle-problems themselves," Hosiah said. "Now 'saved,' busy saving others, making money doing so, they spout virtue. Gotta protect kids, sure, but no low-lifes around *my* Marina."

Granted, his boatyard sat on low ground, out-of-state low- lifes poached his oyster beds and crab lines—Did one of them shoot him?— and Sukie was pregnant "but not from any low- life here. Sukie's guy—"

Sukie's guy lived somewhere around Mudville.

What he'd do tonight was like killing goats, or gooks.

He'd let Mike tell Sukie something like, "Ships sail into sunsets." No pussyfooting with Mike himself, though Edna—

"I'll pour us the pink lemonade we brought," she was saying. "And fry the chops—Protein'll help you heal." Unaware of Hosiah's dietary restrictions, she'd brought lamb chops for the men's lunch.

Only this morning installed in the Marina's cabin-office, he was already entertaining! No more canned gunk to wash down meds. *Real* drink soon as Edna left. His cast-iron pan sputtered on the pot-bellied stove beside the salvaged sink-and- fridge. "So, Mike, let's celebrate. I'm home, and bunking here till...."

"Till what?" Edna unbuttoned her pink raincoat. "Till I cash in my chips, honey, fold my cards."

"Chips! Cards! Sinful waste of time and money," Edna snorted.

He'd not admit launching nightly poker games in the men's ward. An orderly, who confessed his desire to visit Vegas, had rolled beds and wheelchairs around a table, so all the men could reach cards and chips. Damn good rehab, might've kept some of the guys from popping off any sooner…

Edna started sneezing. "Your cabin's maybe clean enough for you, but—"

He kept his cabin-office plenty shipshape! Nobody dusted but who cares? Good county dirt. The orphaned baby goats he'd raised in the cabin still followed him around and were almost housebroken. He expected them to welcome him home now, but the day being muggy, they could still be sleeping.

He'd go outdoors the minute Edna departed and he could fortify himself for the excursion…

***

The day of Hosiah's "accident," Mike had been in the VA hospital for more procedures which didn't seem to have helped much. He, at least, would understand Hosiah's decisions… That night in Nam, when Hosiah carried him bleeding into the FIRST AID tent, Mike said, "When the work you love, doing whatever some god up there or devil below set you down here for, beside a patch of water everyone grew up around, but no longer can you work or screw—You do as they do here, Viet- Cong style." And he'd drawn an invisible knife across his throat, then groped for the scalpel on a nearby towel. Hosiah, quickly slipped the scalpel into the medic's olive green bag, and talked Mike into staying alive. Back stateside, except for bad eyesight, Mike functioned well enough.

Since his stroke, however, Mike couldn't slice butter.

Edna now chopped up his meals, bathed him, doled out his meds, on good days wheeled him to the seawall to drop a line and on rare occasions catch a perch, all with the same protective ardor as she'd brought raincoats today. For this dawn began rosy and an untrustworthy sun appeared for a while, but the day was strangely humid, and the television's weatherman warned thunderstorm.

"You stare at that water," Marianne once observed, "as if you expected Neptune himself to poke his head out of the waves, or a mermaid. Just check the television."

Hosiah didn't need some guy high and dry in some studio to give him any weather report. Through the cabin windows he could see for himself the peculiar platinum sheen on the waves, gulls flying inland, the height of the tide. His knees ached, and from the Marina's flagpoles, two limp red pennants flapped.

Waldo was raising red squares with black centers: small craft warning. "I oughtta be out checking those hawsers myself…".

Mike's milky eyes focused on Hosiah' wheelchair, bandages, leg cast. "Something… wrong?"

"You can't see much of me, but I'm now in the same boat as you: leaky hull half stove-in, unseaworthy. Happened while I was up a mast and Sukie walked into the Marina with her belly like a sail bag—"

Before he could talk about the various follow-ups by detectives who had gone down to the Marina to check out the crime scene, Mike interrupted with the same questions as months before: "How… did you… and Sukie…meet?"

Did Mike really not remember? Might meds erode Hosiah's own memory next? But he didn't mind retelling his stories.

"Before Sukie appeared, five years ago," Hosiah related for the fifth time, "I dreamt being in a field, looking up, m'God, this bundle drops from the sky. Like frogs you read about raining from clouds. Like shrapnel…I searched my dream for a plane. Could be someone fell from the jet trails crisscrossing the sky, those giant tic-tac-toe games the gods play? Shouldn't I duck? The bundle tumbled onto me. Wasn't heavy, but limbs jutted out at angles like that Raggedy Andy. I'd fallen, Mutt, a puppy then, was licking my face, and I was clutching a blanket…Happened night before Sukie appeared."

"Pro-phe-tic," Mike stammered. "Om-en of S-s-sukie and you."

"Nothing ominous about her and me," Hosiah assured him. "The day after that dream—maybe, yeah, prophetic—five years ago, Sukie, wearing a sequined peach tee-shirt and tattered shorts, showed up at the Marina with a spaniel dirty- blond as herself. 'Can't go home,' she bawled, 'They'll punish me for—for blood in my pants! Will I die?"

She was eleven or twelve, not quite sure. Her preacher-parents had just bought the farmhouse uphill. Hosiah escorted her back up the road: nobody home. Yachters and fish boats out all afternoon, Marianne working in her real estate office in Mudville, Edna replenishing craft supplies at Mudville Five-n- Dime, only goats and gulls around, Hosiah, "a graybeard who'd never had children, sure-as-hell didn't want any," had delivered the birds-and-bees lecture.

More interested in his horny goats than in lascivious birds, or bees to which she thought herself allergic, Sukie ran onto the sickle of beach and into the inlet with her spaniel. Mutt, and a docile piebald nanny who wasn't sure swimming was for her, followed. All emerged cleaner until they rolled in the muddy sand. They ran into the water again. Blood washed away, tears forgotten, Sukie led the nanny on a rope up the hill, with Hosiah, Mutt and spaniel trotting in her wake.

"Kin nanny sleep in my closet, Ma? She's real sweet!" "Late! Late again!" Grim as gargoyles her parents yelled,

"Git indoors! Wash! No, you cannot keep that filthy creature!" "I keep my goats clean, Ma'am," Hosiah protested. "I wash my nanny goats' udders daily."

Sukie later told Hosiah her father whacked her ears till they bled, then hosed her with ice water "to cleanse my soul."

Like a stray kitten begging protection—feed it once, yours forever—Sukie kept returning to Hosiah's Marina with her spaniel, and, after "God took him," alone. Hosiah would hardly have tied up the MARIANNE, sold his catch, scribbled in the ledger, stashed whatever cash in a pocket to take to the bank on the morrow, than the girl would appear on his cabin-office porch begging to paint boats or groom goats. He didn't invite her inside: with his wide bunk and double-wide reputation, though he couldn't do much anymore, her Born-Again parents would summon the sheriff. Hosiah stuck to coffee in her presence, handing her a jelly glass of goat milk on the cabin-office steps. She'd rummage in the outside bin for kibbles to feed goats, cats, dogs, sometimes herself. After she headed home, he'd uncork, unscrew or snap open some yachtsman's leftover bottle, or what he'd had to buy himself. Winter nights he splashed rum into a mug of goat milk and warmed it, and he'd sleep better.

Hosiah noticed purple bruises on Sukie's fair skin, and went to see the Special Ed teachers, They too suspected child abuse, "though no preacher would harm anyone." The school principal finally called Social Services. An official knocked at the farmhouse.

"Dumb girl keeps bumping into things, falling down the stairs," her preacher-father said. "Never looks where she's going. Breaks things, makes a mess. Satan punishes her naughtiness. Not right in the head either." Forms signed, the official gone, her father beat Sukie for causing trouble.

Sukie told Hosiah, though he only half-believed her, that when her mother was out, her father wrestled her on the bed and pulled her slacks and panties down. "Father keeps saying 'God, oh God' and maybe he is, but he's real big and it hurts."

"The beatings sure-as-hell what made her nutty," Hosiah said. "So her baby mightn't... inherit...nuttiness, but might pop out bright, like those kids on TV, they're born reading." He sympathized with Sukie's learning problems more than anyone knew. Thanks to what his teachers had labeled an exceptional memory, despite what he'd heard was now called something like "disslecksia," he'd faked it through elementary school. In time he was able to read who had boats or gear to sell, and calculate who owed what.

So he would come up with just another story to tell Sukie.

With her, stories were always new. She needed help with the same homework daily. Hosiah surprised himself recalling arithmetic. Mike, schooled longer, remembered better, until he began forgetting.

Henceforth Hosiah, like Mike, must dig what Marianne once called "realities of infirmities and seaside living." Seasick merely looking at boats, Marianne had set about renting picturesque beach cabins and selling sturdier houses in Mudville. Now that Hosiah really needed her help selling their big useless clapboard house, she'd moved West.

Hosiah was concerned about what to do with Mutt, but maybe if Mike had a dog, like the VA provided some veterans—

"Look at Mutt, Mike," Hosiah said. "Broad chest, solid stance of his Chesapeake Bay retriever sire, rusty coat and friendliness from his Irish setter dam—Real dog, unlike Marianne's toy pouzer what yipped, nipped, shed, shat, ate fancy food…Unlike us, Mutt still runs good…Oh, our lamb chops'll need ketchup—"

Groping in the cabinet, he touched not ketchup but a flat bottle scraped alabaster by decades of tossing on beach pebbles: he kept it full of rum, Waldo had brought the flask to the hospital but, caught trying to sneak it past the nurses, drank it himself, refilled and returned it in Hosiah's cabinet as a welcome home present.

This morning, Hosiah now recounted to Mike and Edna, the ambulance crew, Daisy and Oscar, wheeled the gurney up the ramp and into the cabin. Last July Fourth, Daisy's uncle had chartered the MARIANNE: six passengers plus Daisy and himself, six hours' good fishing even with the fireworks, $600. And they'd left him a six-pack aboard. "You remember good deeds," Hosiah said to Daisy.

"Where's your hospital bed, Captain Hosiah?" she nudged the Marina's tiger cat out of the way. "I thought you'd a wife or something who'd'a ordered one? Wheelchair? Rentals' number on this brochure."

"My bunk'll do fine. M'daddy's wheelchair's in the shed.
I'll just fetch—"

Strange, stuff you inherited, shoulda ditched, from sentiment stowed under tarps, one day yourself needed. Oscar went into the shed and wiped away the spider webs.

From the ambulance they brought—Nothing he'd ever touch: vials of pills and bottles of clear liquid, bedpan (could become Mutt's new water bowl), orange slipper-socks nobody could slip over casts, one week's supply of Ensures—Was he expected to live only a week? He'd take care of things first, let the devil and his goats drink the Ensures. Or Sukie.

As if on cue, Sukie'd appeared, having skipped school again. While the ambulance crew was filling out paperwork, she drank two Ensures, and poured a third into the cats' bowl. The cats lapped it up.

"Hey, aren't you staying at Nurse Annie's in Mudville?" Hosiah asked her.

"Unh-unh."

"Could drive you there—" Daisy volunteered. Thrilled to ride in an ambulance, Sukie gathered her other smock and super-wide jeans. "Hairbrush? Toothbrush?" Daisy reminded her as she stood scrubbing seven jelly glasses, and measuring morphine.

"That's enough to tranquilize Neptune."

"Tomorrow's visiting nurse'll fix the next batch, Captain Hosiah…Big storm due, surprised they dismissed you."

"I've weathered hurricanes, m'dear…"

More important, the sea-glass trophy held rum good as the Jamaican rum in that buried crate. During Prohibition, as the story went, the late Marina owner ran liquor from the Islands to Baltimore for the politicians, made enough to buy some land cheap, stashed some jugs and flasks underground for his own use. In 1929 the Mafia rubbed him out in Miami. Generations later, the bootlegger's descendents turned the warehouse in Mudville into The Purple Turtle, and sold Hosiah the ramshackle Marina and clapboard house. Marianne wanted Swedish modern, so Edna furnished the doublewide with the hand-me-down walnut armoires, four-poster bed, and two red plush Lazy-Boys she covered with antimacassars crocheted herself.

Hosiah, Waldo, and Mike back then in better days, had righted the collapsed piers, repaired the fish-cleaning shed glistening with old fish scales, and shored up the disintegrating boat barn, leaving the owls in residence and swallows' nests mud-glued underneath eaves. They harvested the mussels clinging to algaed pilings, and netted the blue crabs, big jimmies. Hosiah posted ads and boaters flocked for berths and buoys. Since childhood he'd considered motor boats "stink- pots and honey-barges:" their fumes still stank up the air, but their owners paid on time. So Hosiah's Marina prospered.

Digging holes for new fencing to better corral his growing gaggle of goats—he refused to nicker the newborn kids, let the billies grow up and enjoy siring more generations—as an even greater reward their labors, Hosiah's post-hole digger had struck that crumbling crate whose glass bottles of rum remained in fine condition.

Now, Hosiah gathered his energy to visit the pen up the slope. Wheeling that unwieldy chair down the ramp, he passed his garden: rampant rosemary, rapacious ragweed, enormous orange cucumbers. At least the goats would eat them.

Next, he inspected the boatyard: strewn with tatters of yellow cop-tape from the detective's investigations, the same old beer bottles, cans, papers, plastic bags. Down the pier, he could almost see the guano splattering the MARIANNE's decks, the barnacles glommed onto her red hull...Three Monarch butterflies clustered on the milkweed grown tall and blossoming pale pink around the goat pen.

The sky had a storm-coming look...But why not go out with a clap of thunder! He must, however, first feed his goats, check their supply of kibbles, before doing what he had to do.

Suddenly he stopped on the way to the goat pen—who'd look after his goats?

What th'hell—Goat pen empty! Dirt raked clean except for scattered dead leaves. Not a trace of goat...Damn damn damn...Did he not dig the fence posts deep enough? Had his goats escaped because nobody fed them? Had they sickened and...passed away? Or somebody stole—Slumping down in his wheelchair, he held his face in his hands and all but wept.

Marianne gone, The MARIANNE gone. Goats gone. Fish moratoriumed. Crabs and oysters scarce. Summer gone.

Whoever fired that bullet, gone. Health as gone as Mike's. Rum soon gone. Damn damn damn. Better that any clutter of possessions also be gone.

*"In Mudville, Edna honey," Hosiah said, "if you drive near the hospital and that nurse Annie's, or happen upon Sukie's guy somewhere, remind them to drive down tonight. For this TV and some other stuff I won't be needing. On the way, if you see Waldo, ask has he tonged more—" He paused.

Mike rounded his wrinkled lips. "Oysters."

"Yep. This morning when they drove me home to be deep-sixed in a week, Waldo swung by with the season's first. First real breakfast I've had in weeks. Mutt licked the shells." Hearing his name, Mutt licked Hosiah's hand. "You've seen Mutt's smart, Mike. Sukie sometimes feeds him, sometimes forgets. Waldo's allergic. I'd like you to have him. Easy maintenance: fresh water in his bowl and he'll eat leftovers so won't cost you. When he asks, kick open the door. He'll fetch your newspaper and look after you like those companion dogs for disabled veterans. Which you and I are, though from an old war nobody wants to remember. No VA gave us companion dogs."

Mike neck couldn't nod right, but he bobbed his head.

Edna shook her head. "No dogs." She skirted Mutt as if garbage or worse, inspected Hosiah's bandages, realigned jelly glasses. "How d'you manage opening oysters, Ho, you so hurt? And were you allowed them slimy things?"

"Waldo opened them. Slid down our gullets like— oysters."

Hovering over both wheelchairs, twisting her gray curls, Edna unbuttoned, rebuttoned, her raincoat against the storm, whose status the TV kept interrupting football to upgrade. To fill time until she left, Hosiah kept talking. "Remember that New Year's we opened six dozen oysters, Mike, but goats escaped, burst inside, slurped our oysters, drank our eggnog, went prancing across the ice?"

"Can't keep goats in no pen that won't hold water," Edna sniffed. "Remember the Fourth when fireworks spooked your goats, they escaped, invaded everyone's gardens? Your piebald billy ate the preacher's peas, bleated and bloated so bad you slaughtered him, and summer folks phoned 911 about blood in the port so they got the Animal Control inspector to come check."

But the Animal Control inspector had certified that Hosiah's goats were well-tended, and he even rented a slip for his speedboat.

Now, sometime in the last weeks, Hosiah in hospital, someone had stolen his precious goats.

Mike seemed to be studying Hosiah. "Bullet–brain?" Mike's good hand tapped his skull.

"No, here. Not the kind cut out easy. More like buckshot, or shrapnel. Doc thought me asleep when he told Nurse Annie, 'Our captain here faces worse than a smashed pelvis. Please fill these pre-scriptions, give him the usual meds and injections, make him com-fortable. Social Services is locating his sisters or ex-wife to decide whether hospice, or home care, and then what final...'

"Fat chance my ex- or my sisters would care-give me!" Hosiah's much older sisters had told him even when he was small that they'd read that "late babies often have learning problems. Mom was old when you, Hosie, were born, that's why you're slow." His sisters at-tended a "proper" business school, found "proper" jobs, married properly, raised families in proper suburbs, timed babies properly, visited his Marina once. "Awful primitive...Marianne's pretentious, but who'd blame her for leaving?"

"We heard Marianne visited while you were laid up," Edna said.

"She flew in. Nurses reported me asleep, but I overheard her ask them, 'Won't Medicare cover hospice for what little time? No costly lead-lined coffin, pine's fine. Untreated wood disintegrates, like bones.' She's damned ecological! But do bones dissolve fast? Next she said, 'Cremation's earth- friendliest, cheapest.' 'Could you take his clothes home to wash?' the nurses asked. She hesitated but finally with thumb and forefinger picked up the plastic bag with the bloody mess...She must've dumped it at Mudville Laundromat, then she saw our old lawyer, picked up the clothes and returned them clean, flew home."

Burning's out, ladies. No deep-digging me in, either— Even dead, I'd get clausto-whatever cooped up…Meantime, no family's gonna care-give me or clean up afterward. I sure as hell won't hang on in hospices half-crocked on pills. But I've taught Waldo and even Sukie though she forgets, gotta leave things shipshape…

Hosiah seared the chops in the skillet. "I'm managing fine on my own, thanks, Edna. Look! From this wheelchair, I reach coal for the potbelly, strike Lucifers through the dust, grease the skillet.…Pass this on to Sukie too."

"Give that dumb girl this good skillet?" Edna grasped it with a frayed gray towel. "She'd burn holes through cast iron. No wonder the school put her in Special Ed, can't even spell her name. She comes to me crying, can't understand why, when she came home with that big belly, her mother screamed 'whore!' and locked her out. You'da thought they'da taught her certain facts-of-life. Even her full name."

"Sukie's folks are ornery," Hosiah agreed. "But Susannah Kelling-wood Underton is a gutleful. And she can remember the songs Mike in good years taught her. Like Marianne memorizing poems—she'd recite one about going down to the sea in ships…You can't never forget the sea. In hospital I worried would I see oceans again…"

Mike hummed, mumbled something about "mare" and "day-boosi."

"You kin thank us church ladies and the angels for praying you home, Ho," Edna was saying, "like we did for Mike. We'll shop for you, like you'd give us by-catch…And pray more for you. But just out of the hospital, should you be eating real food?"

"Realer the better!" What pretty prayer's gonna protect against real bullets? As for angels! Those old days, grown men saw winged things in clouds, read omens in guts, heaped sins on a goat—whimsy gods explained everything. Thunderclouds above my Marina today, no angels in sight, goats stolen, my entrails in knots no sailor could break, gods dealt me a Queen of Spades, and the vestal virgin ain't virgin no more.

"Watch you don't burn them chops, Ho!"

"Don't Ho him, Sugar." Mike's half-white eyes darted from Hosiah to Edna. "Remember, Nam…freaked…him out."

"S'okay," Hosiah said. "Nothing matters, no more.

Always were, will be, wars driving men nuts, though in our war, few mentioned what Marianne called 'discombobulation of the brain.'"

"Marianne loved big words," Edna said.

Hosiah sensed Edna was glad Marianne was ex, though the two had agreed on "Ho's dirty goats" and "those men should curb their words when ladies present." But he'd kept his goats clean, and *damn* , like other useful four-letter words, was everyday man-talk.

He handed Edna his knife. "When you cut up Mike's chop small, I'd appreciate you cutting mine too. Not like the hospital's purees, though—Lost 20 pounds. You're lucky, Mike, Edna feeds you good. Edna Mae: good woman, good boat." Before Mike's stroke, he and Hosiah had repaired the SHIT SHAPE, a third-hand Doral runabout left for repairs and never reclaimed. They scraped barnacles, fixed the engine, Sukie painted the hull blue. Mike was happy with it. Edna remained too mortified to step aboard until, ignoring superstitions against renaming boats, they rechristened her EDNA MAE. Hosiah in his MARIANNE led their flotilla between channel markers, while in his wake Mike steered the EDNA MAE and sang what Edna called his "bare toney aires." Sukie trolled for stripers.

Last Hosiah'd seen the EDNA MAE, guano covered her decks, barnacles her hull, crabs and fish nuzzled the seaweed. "Shame the new owners neglect her, don't know shipshape from—" Sheep shit almost slipped out.

"Here's your chops, fine as hamburger."

"Thanks, Edna…You can leave us alone, honey, we can't run off anywhere."

"Good you're running no more boats to drink on…Now you run bad as Mike, Ho."

"Ummmm. Mike and I are now like those geezers at Mom-'n'-Pop's. They remember the Korean War…Locals or striped-shirt summer geezers, they play cards, talk sports, stocks-on-the-dock, don't entertain new ideas. Forever arguing there ain't been anyone good since Ted Williams or Connie Mack or di Maggio."

"I gotta run before it rains." Edna buttoned her raincoat. "Bought me a cell phone, you've your land line, we'll touch base." She straightened Mike in his wheelchair, smoothed sleeves over his wrinkled arms, and, moving jelly glasses aside, for the third time wiped the galley sink and counter. They'd been plenty clean enough for Hosiah, but even at home, Edna washed everything thrice over, including Mike whether he needed it or not. Now Edna arranged yet another plaid shirt over him, then his raincoat. "Bye-bye baby, don't talk too much…Ho, you'd be lucky to get two words outta my old codger today."

"We've gotten each other's words out for fifty years, Edna. We enlisted together, raised hell together, shipped out, met up, fought and bitched together. When that mine exploded in Nam, I lugged him to FIRST AID. He's picked me up when I've— Both now— codgers—we retell tales, bore you."

"'Course not," Edna protested, though Hosiah knew her a godly woman who'd swallow sea serpents rather than speak evil.

"Sorry you can't stay, honey," Hosiah said. "Caretakers need time-out. Hospital nurses take breaks whenever everyone's buzzing to wake the dead."

"You need nurses here, Ho. You think you can cook. How you gonna bathe, shave?"

"My beard'll return. Can bathe myself, just haven't tried yet." Bathing had been simple matter, before: if sweaty and fishy, he'd dive overboard, then run the Marina's outdoor shower over himself. For winters, the big house had bathrooms. Now, of course, he couldn't get there. But the marina had a privy just back of the cabin, sponge baths in the galley sink would suffice. If he stank of hospital, he'd soon take care of unsightly looks and smells for good. Only a matter of navigating the damn wheelchair.

Meanwhile, he'd locate that rum. "A man needs liquid to wash down supper, right, Mike? Our daddies set the example."

Both born near Mudville, Mike's family moved inland for him to attend a better high school and a nearby music academy. By chance meeting again before signing up for Vietnam, they served together during the war, once more becoming buddies. When after Mike's injury, when he was fit again but for his eyes, weekdays he'd worked at his father's MUDVILLE MARINE, supplying Hosiah at cost, and on good weekends took the bus down to crew on the MARIANNE. He joined the local chorus and, barely able to decipher the scores, quickly memorized the music. When doctors couldn't repair his eyes further, he and Edna, the firm's office lady, bought the doublewide, rooting it uphill from the Marina. She'd convinced Mike of a church wedding, encouraged him to join the choir, and didn't mind his fishing all day, first in Hosiah's MARIANNE, then his own EDNA MAE, until his stroke hit.

Now Edna doubled shawls over them. "Will you be warm enough? Weather's changing. I'll check in…Bye-bye, Sugar Pie." And she took off.

At last! They could relax. "Good to be with old friends," Hosiah said. "I didn't feel old before…the shooting."

"Me neither…not before…before my stroke." Mike spoke almost clearly.

Two years ago, Mike was struck down. Dumbly, in Hosiah's opinion. Edna hadn't cut up his steak. Mike often talked with his mouth full, bursting into song to illustrate a point. One chunk didn't go down his throat. Edna screamed from the doublewide. Hosiah sprinted up the slope. While she was frantically redialing 911, he squeezed Mike's ribs as waiters supposedly did with greedy eaters. The chunk stuck. The ambulance crew arrived, cleared Mike's throat, sirened him to Mudville hospital, Hosiah and Edna following in his pickup.

Doc Scoples' diagnosis: "Brain damage." Weeks in VA rehab barely helped. Hosiah almost prayed then.

In fair weather, before Edna set off to sell her jam and antimacassars at CROSSROADS PRODUCE, she'd wheel Mike to the bulkhead. Clutching a rod fastened to his wheelchair, his right hand fixed slippery clams on hooks, reeled in the line. The Marina's regulars removed any catch, or if it rained, wheeled him indoors. Even Sukie watched him; if she drifted off, Mutt herded her back. Mike always thirsty, Edna bungeed jugs of ice-water to the wheelchair. Regulars refilled them at the Marina's pump. As soon as Hosiah returned from fishing, sold his catch and put the MARIANNE to bed, he'd fetch beers from The CRABSHACK, or as the guys called it, the CRAB-SHIT. The men would cool down or warm up according to season.

Was he now reduced to the same damn half-life? Hosiah imagined Sukie, baby carriage nearby, supposedly watching both wheelchairs, Waldo checking from the boat yard, Edna returning to fuss over them.

Hosiah spat in the stove, listened to the brief sizzle. How many hours left today?

"Take…boats out again…?" Mike asked, apparently recalling their last expedition, last May, before the Marina got busy. Gulls diving for the bluefish running beyond the lighthouse, Hosiah took an old cottage-cheese container of bait from the galley fridge and he, Edna and Sukie lifted Mike, wheelchair and all, for a final ride aboard the EDNA MAE. Edna brought tuna sandwiches and lemonade. Everyone landed two stripers before they again interrupted poachers working Hosiah's trot lines, netting his crabs. He cranked up the ship-to-shore for Marine Police. After the poachers chugged away, shouting they'd be back so better watch out, a patrol boat appeared.

The other problem that day was Sukie, never seasick, vomiting overboard.

"Much slips my mind," Mike was saying, in a firmer voice. "Not just… where yesterday I misplaced keys to my pickup and the house keys. How did Sukie…meet…her guy?"

Hosiah knew Mike hadn't driven in years, and for years he'd told Mike about Sukie's guy. But hell, he'd repeat the story. "The guy's a bricklayer. Building the school's courtyard, singing as he worked, lured Sukie over at recess. She started singing with him, and carrying bricks. 'Had to help, lotta bricks, not heavy if you take one in each hand. I counted every one. He's promised me jobs doing his A-counts'."

"Sukie…with…accounts?"

"She cut Special Ed because numbers made no more sense than letters. Her teachers decided she was learning something counting bricks, measuring flowerbeds, writing with a carpenter's pencil. They gave up fussing, and afternoons checked her out with other children lined up for the school busses. Sukie still wait for her guy's motorcycle.

"Gotta help him build our house," she explained. "He can't afford pipes yet, can't swipe more boards from other jobs, so we can't move in yet. He pulls the mattress onto the cement, and we sorta nap." By six p.m., he got her home and zoomed back to Mudville. Building other houses, he was always finishing theirs on empty land near the town Dump.

"Let trash men handle spoiled goods," Sukie's father said. "May she burn in Hell for her sins."

Sukie had no sins nor sense of sin, Hosiah was damn sure.

He wondered if the future house were ever going to be ready, despite the details she provided. Meanwhile she still hung around the Marina, and even while getting rounder, she curried goats, scaled and gutted catch, tossed the entrails to the cats.

With Eco-detergent, brushes and rags, she detailed people's trucks and boats, and repainted Mike's EDNA MAE. A streaky paint job, all the more so as Sukie had used red anti-fouling paint supposed to be for bottoms for the whole hull, but the new owner from the city only wanted a party boat for weekends and a red hull was fine with him.

"In the hospital," Hosiah told Mike, "I finalized selling my MARIANNE to Waldo. He'll take on Sukie's guy. My blessed oyster boat for twenty-five years since my Daddy passed. What money Waldo left for me, we'll set aside for Sukie. What else would I be saving the money for?"

Mike squinted at Hosiah, then toward the Marina, where the EDNA MAE's new owner had moored her to the wrong buoy. "Bad...bad... bad." Mike could have meant his eyesight, the new skipper's seamanship, either man's condition, or the whole lot.

Burrowing as far back in his fridge as he could reach from the damn wheelchair, Hosiah found moldy goat cheese flecked with green. He'd supplied everyone who'd drink goat milk.

When the milk tasted of rosemary and garlic grass, Edna made herbed goat cheeses for her CROSSROADS PRODUCE. Little market for gourmet delicacies except among summer folk.

When October turned stormy, Edna stashed the rest in his fridge. This must be the last of it.

Hosiah mourned his goats. What in hell had happened to them? He'd sue someone to get them back. A job for the cops, though they hadn't caught whoever had shot him.

With Sukie and the goats, he could talk all he wanted, though either might meander off before he finished a paragraph. Goat udders became the only tits left to hang onto.

The air was increasingly heavy, gathering strength for later. At least Sukie was safe at the nurse's till her time... Time...Every minute counted when only so many left. Mike still automatically checked his bare wrists. Hosiah's watch ruined in the fall from the brig, he could only guess how much remained of this day, how many pills, how many inches in the jelly glasses he sipped only enough to dull the pain. He reached for the sea-glass flask, uncorked it and splashed rum in their mugs. He wasn't sure he could lift a full kettle but at least the bottle was lighter.

Mike sipped the rum. "Thank…"

"Good dining with you, Mike. You can't see but dimly, mostly croak like a sea robin, but you're talking today. Smell the garlic Edna won't use? Can you see outside?"

Sea-glass bottles blocked any clear view. Hosiah had retrieved the century-old flasks one low tide, and, like a bowerbird gathering shiny objects to impress a mate, thought to please Marianne.

"The barnacles make them—artistic…But dirty old bottles in-doors?" She'd aligned them on his office windowsills. Sunlight through the glass, moonlight or the Marina's security light, turned the dusty blue, green and brown glass iridescent.

Hosiah kicked open the cabin door, turned their wheelchairs so he and Mike could watch the storm billowing in. Thunderheads loaded down the sun, pushing it under waves of clouds. No angels up there. Beyond the splintery windowsill, boats were bobbing in their slips, tugging at their buoys. Had Waldo double-checked their hawsers before he took off to deliver oysters to Mudville Market? The wind slammed the door shut. Lightning flashed. Mutt scrambled under the table.

The goats never liked storms either…

"Our daddies knew weather, when to head to port, where to find bars. And ladies! After Ma passed, I'd wake before school, find one 'auntie' after another at our kitchen table, crushing her cigarette butts into Ma's favorite blue-and-white saucer, you've seen it around, with a fisherman standing on a bridge. Didn't the thrift-shop lady call it willow ware? Ma'd never allowed smoking."

"Like Edna…House…goddess…"

"You and I were gods of the sea once, Mike…All this storm build-up will only end in one de-ci-sive clap and flash. How much of a gale or war or death is the wait?"

"For the more. Or no-more…Waiting hard, hanging onto walker, bed, wheelchair." Mike had become well-nigh loquacious with the rum. "Your hand-me-down bootlegger's four-poster fills half our doublewide…Edna calls it marriage bed. How… Marianne and you… now?"

"Guess we're on friendly terms, continent between us…She took off…"

Intuitive as an animal, before the last tropical storm three years ago, Marianne had packed up her family silver, clothes, suitcases, laptop, and picked up her silly dog who at the first thunderbolt scrambled under the bed. She kissed Hosiah's forehead. "You're a stubborn old waterman, and it's too complicated to live in intimate proximity with you. Still, I'm fond of you. But enough of picturesque seaside living for me. Hurricanes jinx real estate sales. I'm selling the business, and moving inland to some decent suburban neighborhood with space for children and my books." She'd set off in her laden red convertible first only as far inland as Mudville Motel. For weeks after she'd moved to town, she'd drive to the Marina for striped bass or whatever he'd cleaned, gave her free, and she could cook in the motel kitchenette.

"As close to alimony as I could get—dead fish."

As for children, Hosiah couldn't imagine even one child.

Preoccupied now closing shutters, pulling boats to the barn and goats to the shed, he had no more time to mull over distractions like potential progeny.

Now the television was warning citizens to stock up and move into an emergency shelter inland: this would be a serious tropical storm. Edna phoned that everyone was safe in Mudville's emergency shelter, and she'd be back soon to pick up the men. Yes, Sukie was safe with Nurse Annie. She spotted Waldo already standing by at the volunteer fire department.

Looking out the door, Hosiah could see guys at CRAB SHACK boarding up the big windows, and, Hank the owner, and the help preparing to leave. En route Hank stopped by the cabin to ask if the men didn't want a ride into Mudville—

"No? You may be getting a ride in a few minutes? But here, take today's bread we won't be using—Oh, your goats? I'd seen that foreigner stop before, wanting goats to sell for Greek Easter. Must have given County Animal Control his card. Wop or wog or mic, anyway from elsewhere. I have nothing against them folks, mind you, but while you were in hospital, that foreigner lassoed them while Animal Control's van waited, rear doors open. Animal Control officers and the foreigner herded your goats into the van. Impounded because— here, read the document they left at CRABSHACK, *Unlawful to keep livestock in a gentrified seaside village.*

"Me and you and the goats," Hosiah fumed, "we were here when this was only a seaside village and gentry meant the GENTS at your CRAB SHACK and nobody asked for—" his voice rose to falsetto– "'Pomegranate margarita, please.' Damn glad my goats shat up their damn white van."

"Yeah, seems when the van sat in the County yard, doors not tight and the hood up, the goats butted their way out and chewed through the electric system. One billy electrocuted himself but the rest escaped and scattered, chomping their way through the County's landscaping and people's petunias. But we gotta get on up the road before it washes out—"

"Good! But boats or goats," Hosiah sighed, "I can't herd neither now. Damn, power's off…No, on again…Off again."

"I'll procure a bigger vehicle in Mudville, Captain Ho,"

Hank said. "Then I'll hurry back here to get you guys and your wheelchairs to Mudville."

Likely on the way stopping at Mudville's Purple Turtle, open as late as customers bought drinks.

Lightning flashed, thunder crashed, the cats flashed their orange-striped behinds and disappeared, but Mutt remained across Hosiah's feet. This time Edna phoned that their pickup's rusted muffler fell off when she went over a curb, but she'd locate Sukie's guy who'd said he had extra auto parts, and though she was frantic to get back to Hosiah and Mike, her hairdresser insisted that she stay overnight at her house in Mudville. Officer Tom Brenton stopped by to check on them, then was off to set up barricades on the shore road. Soon as Animal Control's van was free, he'd drive down retrieve the men in their wheelchairs.

"We're shipshape here," Hosiah insisted on the phone. "Flashlights, Coleman lanterns, Strike Anywheres, canned beans and sardines, jugs are full of fresh water." Other bottles contained what Edna called "fire water." Best way to kill pain and survive any storm.

Again Edna phoned. Mike began to sing Good Night Ladies, and with his good hand, clicked the receiver down.

"Eat up, Mike, drink up," Hosiah said. "Power'll go soon, so no TV. Let's check Weather again, though it's not like I told Sukie, gods bowling up there." He'd make their acquaintance soon enough.

Mike looked around, reached awkwardly for the old juice bottle in the wheelchair's saddlebags. Hosiah had ditched his father's plastic piss bottles, but wished they both had them now, not the uncomfortable bedpan.

"Like that fat-assed brig we're fixing for the museum folks, you and I are—Hey, let's take a leak out the door the way we did as kids and our mothers yelled we were 'worse'n trailer trash.' Edna and Marianne got pissed off too.... My feet'll steer you to the door, then it's a clear shot...C'mon, Mutt, you too...Already starting to rain light, but soon it'll pour like hell out there...Back to safe harbor soon's we're done." Hard against the wind, Hosiah opened the cabin door. Afterwards exhausted, he needed another pick-me-up. "Another little drink won't do us any harm—' You used to sing something like this...Wait, that's *my* glass of what the doctors gave me, a double dose now, your mug's by your other hand...We'll get smashed tonight, if not as smashed as before shipping out, again when we'd hit port. Smashed but alive then, with more to fork than lamb chops..."

Tonight he'd walk out from the Marina Beach...He'd have to wait till someone came by to pick up Mike but then he, Hosiah, would walk to the shore and keep going...

Wind came up and rain increased. Power died and didn't come on again. The storm struck full force—

The power and the glory of it! Hosiah imagined the big clapboard house up the hill shaking and cracking, while real branches and maybe trees crashed, and in the Marina—He hoped the few boats still in the water, above all his MARIANNE, wouldn't break their hawsers and crash against the pier or the jetty which delineated the port. The cabin shuddered, plates fell and broke, shingles and window glass shattered. But these jerrybuilt walls held, this roof did not even leak the way the roof always did in the big house. Surely leaking buckets up there now.

Mike was more-or-less humming some tune.

"Me, I wouldn't know one note from another," Hosiah said. "Wish I— Sukie turns up singing hymns or Country, shows me a score she sings from. So she's not a hundred percent retard. Music easier than schoolwork. After one hearing, she sings commercials from TV all too well." Most of what they touted, insurance and silky shampoos and machine- made freezer dinners, he didn't need. Only the storm was selling itself tonight.

Officer Brenton wasn't making it to the Marina, nor would any visiting nurse. "We're fine on our own, aren't we, Mike…Another sip?"

***

By the next mid-morning, rain stopped though wind kept on. Mutt ran out barking, a wan sun appeared, electricity and the phone worked again. Edna called. "How are you, Sugar? I worried so hard! Soon as someone clears the trees across the streets I'll be back, restore order."

"Don't worry, honey, we're doing fine," Hosiah assured her.

Since Mike was still asleep in his chair, Hosiah wheeled his own to the porch, down the slippery ramp, over the soggy grass and around the cabin to see his pear tree uprooted.

Worse, he could see up the hill the big pin-oak fallen across the clapboard house! Stove it in! He wheeled through the rubble.

The few items intact included another cast-iron skillet, a bucket, a chamber pot, pieces of a smashed television set. Damned pity Marianne hadn't managed to sell the house to someone. Whatever buyer would be cursing the destruction mightily today, but he'd have had the income in time to bank it as well as pay hospital bills, and whatall repairs to the Marina, these would cost a fortune. How'll I get by anyway? Boat sold, can't fish but at the bulkhead like Mike, though he doesn't catch but not quite legal-size spot and perch. So, livelihood and health gone…Gotta attend to whatever gotta attend to first…

Hosiah wheeled around the Marina. The pier had lost fish-cleaning shed and gas pump overboard, but Waldo and Sukie's guy together could raise them. The boat barn was flooded a foot deep, but walls stood. Up the slope, the goat shed built of cement blocks, and the flimsy doublewide held: the heavy furniture from the bootlegger's house must have anchored it. The cats reappeared. Hosiah poured a can of Ensure into a pie tin, and they lapped it up..

Mike didn't wake up even when Hosiah brewed coffee.

Yep, they'd put away a lotta rum.

By noon, several boat owners came to survey the storm- torn Marina and stopped into the office. One man promised his outmoded laptop for the cabin-office, another brought Hosiah and Mike sandwiches and a six-pack. Alas, the rum was gone, but Hosiah gratefully snapped the tabs on a couple of cans.

Mike wasn't interested in the sandwiches or the beer.

Tomorrow the cabin would become Waldo's Marina office. TV could wait for Sukie's guy to fetch it. "Gotta remind him, remember the remote. Aren't you glad, Mike, for the oversized screen I bought for the cabin? Better than the old set left in the big house, though that works good too. Hurricane trashed everything up there…Guess even so you can't see any picture but halfways, though you hear good…and you sure can hear wind still roaring out there, banging the shutters."

Hosiah couldn't figure how to say goodbye to Sukie or Edna; shreds of manners intimated he should. He fumbled for his tobacco pouch in the drawer. No pipes allowed in the hospital, but reaming now, scraping, dumping, refilling, tamping, striking matches, gave a man time to think. "I know you too hurt like hell, Mike. We both do. Before Edna returns, we could help that—Remember last Christmas when Waldo's nephew brought that grass? The stuff made my head twist into crazy shapes, doubling, ballooning like pink bubble gum, but helped you. The rest is stashed in this drawer. When they were hauling me out of the hospital, Doc, as if he knew I'd try, warned, 'None of that kid stuff with your meds.' Now I've ditched the meds, I'll retry the stuff…What will happen with Sukie?"

Hosiah poured the lukewarm coffee in the mugs, inhaled deeply. "Time's come to lower my sails, Mike, pitch anchor, stow gear for good. Maybe, stuck as you are too, you'll be envious how I manage… That lawyer, whose yacht we winched into the boat barn last month, he phoned to say Marianne had just phoned him to ask if he'd check my old will she'd made me write, it left her everything, was it still valid! After the bills, won't have much to leave anyone except what's in trust for Sukie. The lawyer and Mudville bank will dole it out to her." Hosiah rinsed the skillet to keep flies off the grease, always some slipped in, late September. "I showed Sukie you can't use those industrial-strength scourers on cast iron, you take a paper towel with cooking oil so pans don't rust."

Mutt nosed around. "Okay, last bits of lamb in my chair, gristle," Hosiah continued. "For a while, Sukie can keep him in their new place…But she'll be busy with her kid, might forget the dog. Instinct'll make her nurse when the baby cries, or her breasts will leak, and remind her. Breasts like that figurehead's. C'on, Mike, pat Mutt's head. You need a watchdog, Edna complains things disappear from your doublewide. I know you suspected Sukie after she painted your kitchen, till I convinced you that girl hadn't the sense to swipe anything except candy if it sat out. Not with all Ten Commandments beaten into her by that Born-Again daddy, though he musta forgot Thou-Shalt-Nots against fornicating. D'you remember any commandment about that? Gotta multiply! Sukie's daddy wouldn't like us drinking neither, would he!" Hosiah was glad he could still entertain Mike with talk, just as with Sukie. But God, he hurt.

Rum gone, he turned to the row of jelly glasses, from which he'd caught Mike sipping yesterday.

"When Sukie saw me last week, all twisted, bandaged, my hair gone patchy white, she told me her father said God was punishing me for my sins. She asked were my sins like what her father said hers were, 'fornikitting?' Was I crocheting pink-and- blue blankets? Yeah, though I wouldn't talk like that to her, indeed I used to 'fornickittate' till my prostate unraveled. As Great Uncle Bert from Texas used to say, not original with him—wasn't 'an original thinker,' guess I inherited that gene— 'I like my coffee strong, my whiskey straight, horses fast, women wild.' Now that damn bullet's tied my parts in sheep's- head knots, Doc can't knit me back. Oxycontin and morphine barely help." Mike still didn't answer but Hosiah kept on talking. "Didn't Edna tell you any details about my accident?

Hell—we got beers, let's drink to Sukie's unborn…"

What if her guy brings her to visit and things start happening here? What do people do in such crises, boil water? "Whatinhell would I doing helping to deliver anything more than a goat? No offspring I know of, none to will the Marina to. My sisters hate it here so I sure won't will anything to them. No goats to will anyone…."

Power on and off while up the road, the electric co-op's cherry-picker was fixing the wires. But you don't have to see to drink. Let it get dark, so I can't see you, Mike, clearly, with your screwed-up face and limbs. Easier that way to remember when you were okay…

Hosiah knew Sukie would eventually forget his existence, or nonexistence. At least he'd not to have to say goo-goo to any baby or recite dumb fairy tales. But is Sukie able of teach her kid anything? She still begs for stories about sailing the high seas, a phrase she must have picked up somewhere, though she's picked up little else. As for "sailing the high seas, kiddo, I'm sailing off tonight, high as I can get."

Hosiah sipped at a glass. Overnight, though he didn't remember drinking any, rum had been enough to put him to sleep, the levels had all dropped pretty far. Like the tide in the Marina now the storm was over, so half the harbor was muddy sand. Could he manage the fat wheelchair on the narrow pier?

The television came on again full blast. The screen flickered, two minutes later died again. The landline phone would be on and off too.

"Navigate over, Mike, you still turn faucets good enough…If you're real thirsty, reach your good arm, must be another bottle somewhere…I'm hurting midships." He gave Mike's wheelchair a kick toward the sink. "Imagine, five years ago I inherited a child, now she's popping a child. 'Imminent.' Doc warned, had to explain 'imminent'. I double-checked it in Marianne's old dictionary…Sukie's guy better finish that house quickly…Hey, Mike, tell Waldo when you see him, keep my pickup too, okay? And Mike, you can be damn sure I'm not going to any hospice with those sick old people popping off right and left. Starboard and port. Everyone clusters around to escort you to death like some big Italian wedding on TV…Me, I'll get to death on my own. Damn…my guts again. The hospital doles pain pills like Lifesavers. They'd wake me to give me another. The way they did when you had your stroke. Doc warned pills addictive—Oxycontin, and I get wild dreams.

Wish I ad them now, didn't take any yet today, but saved a bunch…Yeah, Mike, we've had good lives, right? Women come and go but good watermen stick together like oysters' bivalves…Rum really musta got to you, Mike! But sleeping it off's good. My nights in the hospital, I didn't sleep till three a.m. then stayed groggy all day till naptime. If I'd had rum—"

But in those seconds before sleep came, his mind's eyes might start off seeing friends, the fisherman down the wharf whom he only knew as Joe, the itinerant carpenter who gave his name as Tank, any number of girls whose names he forgot.

People morphed into blobs, blurred, dissolved. That was maybe how he'd morph into death, slipping neatly from visions into blobs into nothing—Might be instants of splitness, as when the moon got caught in the pear tree, hooked on a branch—But it could be a good hooking, a good hooker-sort of hooking—

"Mike, remember how Doc used to prescribe us cold pills. 'Take two Coricidin, have a good lay, sleep well, morning you'll feel fine.' Lotsa hungry city divorcees and wives tanning their legs and boobs on the dock in the old days, happy to engage us in conversation. Anxious husbands kept their shotguns clean for more than the unlucky deer. Or, anxious to do their own thing again off in Mudville, Hubbie maybe didn't care what Wifee did…Those were the days, weren't they! Edna watched you didn't ogle them too close…with what eyesight you had left… Marianne kept a sharp watch too. Now she's gone—too late for us to screw around Mudville."

Mike might be quietly snoring, though it was hard to be sure, given the wind rattling everything.

"Lotsa time in hospital to figure things out," Hosiah continued. "Bad enough, those flowered gowns that split up the stern."

Television and lights came on again, then the phone rang. "Damn, Edna can't leave us alone…No, Sukie's guy…"

Hosiah clicked on the Speakerphone so Mike could hear too. "… Can't make it down today, Captain Ho, but I'll send a buddy. How much the set worth? Gonna need money fast—No, Sukie's at that nurse's. Storm tore a section off my roof, still raining like crazy here…But I'm outta the weather… Somewhere more or less else… Gotta talk fast, sorry for the background noise. I need a bunch of money–"

The phone went dead. Lights flickered out. Hosiah shook the receiver, then the bottle. He definitely now was convinced Sukie's guy

had a wife and kids in the next town, Sukie merely his afternoon di-
version. Hosiah was in no mind to give money to him, nor directly
to Sukie who would. He'd talk with that lawyer when the phone
worked again.

"So let's have another drink, Mike. Edna won't be here anytime
soon. Toothpaste by the sink before she comes...Make sure it's Sukie,
not her guy, or Marianne, what gets Waldo's money from the MAR-
IANNE, the pickup and the Marina. Put it away just for Sukie's kid.
When Waldo brought us oysters, he also left cash in that sail bag in
the starboard cabinet. He'll drive me to the bank later to deposit.
Can't have it sitting around—"

The television and lights in the cabin were off again, electricity
couldn't make up its mind. Now he could see clouds blowing back,
a lightness in the sky.

"Look outside, Mike, only big wind now." Mike's head was
lolling more on his chest. "Yep, we stayed up all night drinking and
talking while the rain and wind argued out there."

Hosiah wheeled to the door, kicked it open. Rain gone, light
flooded in with a few mosquitoes. Out in the harbor, boats still jerked
at their hawsers, but seemed less agitated. He sat looking out, pissed,
dozed, finally opened his eyes to see a figure coming through the
scruffy grass. Waldo?

Edna. He straightened, dumped his glass onto the pile of dis-
carded oyster shells beside the ramp, wheeled back to the sink for
toothpaste.

"Hi, honey, we're fine. Mike's ready to go—asleep already."

"Ho," Edna began, "before I give you some news, given that
storm, I'm gonna need another day in Mudville to get my hair done.
Wednesday? You free to sit Mike then?"

"Sure...We'll ask Waldo if he'd tong more oysters and, as the
striped-shirters would say, the three of us'll batch it in style. Hey,
Mike, say hello to Edna. Power's on, you can watch the shows. Still
sleeping it off?"

Mike remained slumped in his wheelchair, his usually stiff neck forward, quiescent expression on what was visible of his face.

"Here's the news," Edna said. "Sukie's guy got caught swiping copper wire and stacks of shingles from a job—He's behind bars now. When the storm struck, Sukie went into false labor but's back at the nurse's, asked me to ask you if the police tracked down who fired that bullet at you."

"Haven't been out investigating. Cops were doing the usual follow-ups, but far as I know, no clues. They've probably lost interest, the case'll go cold by itself."

"And Sukie's parents," Edna continued, "told the hospital what told Nurse Annie, they've arranged for the adoption."

"God, no, Edna! Sukie loves that baby already! She's come up with twenty names, keeps saying how they'll take it to the new house. As if…I'll give her what's left of the clapboard house…Her guy can repair it…they'll let him out in time…." "What's left of the clapboard house probably in better shape than what Sukie's guy was supposedly building for them. I just drove past his site. Mostly still scaffolding. Sugar, wake up!"

"Yeah, Mike, gotta hear about Sukie's guy." "You boys were drinking! Can smell it on you!"

"Those lamb chops we marinated in summer folks' leftover burgundy kept dripping down our chests."

"Mike's shirt—all wet."

"Plaid won't stain." Hosiah's mind remained on Sukie's goddamned guy. "Mike'll wake up while you're bouncing him home over the ruts, though it's muddy out there."

Edna sniffed her fingers in the dusk. "Not wine, hard stuff! Shame on you, Ho! I don't dare leave him with you again! Sit up, Sugar, gotta hit the road."

Hosiah looked around the cabin. He hurt. Whereinhell was what Daisy had poured in the jelly glasses for him, was it morphine maybe?

Edna began screaming. "His throat's cut! Lord have mercy! His throat—Call 911—Fast—Help! Helllllllp!"

"Goddamn it, Edna! Stop shrieking!! Hand me your phone!"

The operator was taking forever to come on the line: downed trees, downed wires, highway accidents.

Edna kept screaming, "How am I going to—"

Didn't matter if Edna meant, how was she going to save Mike, or how she'd survive without a husband to tend, or how would she explain his "accident." Any way but suicide.

"Mike, Mike, what've you gone and done, what've you done to all of us…Edna, the ambulance will come…Forgive us, Edna… And forget me. I'm heading out to sea."

Hosiah knew he'd never live down the anguish. Edna would manage to find someone to look after. He still held her cell phone to his ear, trying to hush her so he could hear the 911 operator. His free hand wiped at Mike's chin and neck, his bloodied fingers checked for pulse on Mike's good hand still clutching the filet knife.

Screaming, Edna grabbed the handles and began pushing Mike's wheelchair down the cabin ramp, up and over the muddy lane to the road, where the now-useless ambulance was supposed to meet them.

Mike's blood still reddening his hands, Hosiah let his own wheelchair roll down the ramp from the cabin over the soggy mud and sand to the edge. The water gleamed gray but calm as if the storm had never churned it into surf. Still, underneath, incoming tide swirled muddy onto the muddy sickle of beach.

The wheel chair slowed and threatened to suck itself into the mud. Mustn't get mired in the mud meeting my Maker! Hey, illiteration, Marianne might call it. He propelled himself along, his good foot pushing.

Shadows overhead flicked across the Marina. Gulls were flying back, now the storm had passed. Vultures! Two, sweeping, swooping, the gray on black shoulders and wings gleaming. Damn it, be gone! Don't land here yet! Give me a few more hours!

He must stick around until Sukie's parents, finally admitting they were grandparents, took her back with the baby. He guessed that meanwhile, till the big clapboard house was repaired, he'd have to let her move back to the cabin with—it.

Not that he liked baby noises, but who else could teach the kid to hammer together a skiff, bait a hook with slippery squid, remove a fish without skewering his hands on the dorsal fins?

Mutt stretched up and put his head on Hosiah's lap. Who could tend Mutt right?

Wotthehell, isn't Edna now free to look after them…?

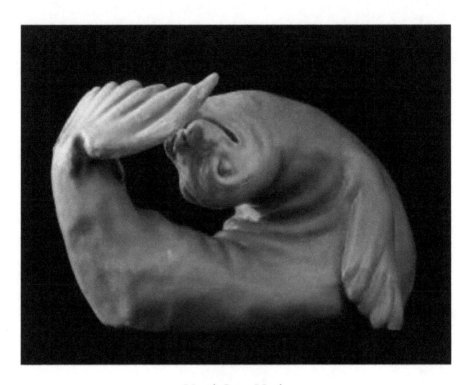

Head Over Heels

Material: Ceramic
Size: 10H x 10W x 12D

The Traveler Meets Her Double in the Balkans

YOU CLAIM you were fated to be my double.

Among rubies unglued from diadems and epaulettes torn off cashiered generals, in the museum, we meet by chance, talk, rush to board the same bus, sit side by side. You are tall, hair light brown, high cheekbones, fine nose, a scarf wound three times around your neck. You are glad to practice your English, interspersed with words hard to decipher.

We ran for the same bus across the mountains, now share the only empty double seat.

You read my palms, decode my eyes, insist, "We are twins, fraternal, got lost from each other. A long time already you live among us."

I answer, "But I've barely arrived—"

Yet our Slavic genealogies are mirror images, our histories as if carved on one birch tree...And I have studied your country.

A different world you inhabit now, your politics, beliefs, non-beliefs, are not mine. Still, you are hospitable, I am polite.

Flat tire! The bus halts by a river. I explore down a path.

You scratch stanzas on the cold sickle of sand, in verses you claim unravel our supposed futures together. I barely decipher your words...

Tire repaired, the driver resumes our journey. The bus swerves around curves—We cushion each other. Your warmth envelops me like mist. Throughout the corkscrew mountain drive, you argue ideologies. I disagree with your ideas: my forbearers suffered too much under such regimes. Yet, a guest in your land, I listen politely, nod, and doze.

The road dissolves in marigolds. The bus stops by a church. Passengers descend. You grab your backpack, I mine. We touch the dusk of chapel walls, troop inside. Two crones in black, like prunes, recite their toothless prayers. They collect our coins for tawny candles which, from other candles stuck in sand on a small altar beneath the icon of a hoary saint, we light to honor gold-framed icons painted with swarthy martyrs and smoky Madonnas. They watch darkly while we bend to kiss the patchwork bones of boxed-in saints.

I am surprised by your devoutness in this officially godless country, wonder why you take the risk, wonder that the bus has brought us here.

Suddenly your basso chants the almost-familiar mass in Old Slavonic! In this officially godless land! Your chanting lifts me through high onion domes—I am crying into the slit of sky. My tears become sparrows in the eaves.

"My grandfather in his later years became a monk," you explain, and so that the other passengers overhear, but nobody reports you for suspect liberal ideas, you lecture me on forbidden nobility, dangerous religion.

Outside the church again, I shiver with the unexpected cold. The priest hands me a pomegranate, a nun pours fire in gold-rimmed thimble glasses and only for us. She asks if we are related, and tucks one glass in my purse, signs the cross over us both. *Why us*, I wonder, *not over all the rest ...*

Outside the church, the world smells rosemary. We cross the cobblestones to a café under grapevines. The wine is red, the bread brown, stuffed peppers red and green, lamb chops grilled black on the open fire, a pomegranate for dessert.

You write a poem on a napkin:
>*Beware the traitor beside you,*
>   *believe in the blind, trust the fool.*

"What do you know of death?" you ask.

"My brushes with death? Unspectacular encounters.

Undertow greedy off Rio, camouflaged amanitas, a typhoon somersaulted my plane over Manila. Nothing much. I survived.

You surely risked your life in this land of invasions, militia, guerrillas, famine, TB? A handsome child-partisan you must have been!"

"I? No…See that mutt in the dust? His tail forms a question mark. Let me throw him your bone…Here, we all are grateful for foreign aid."

This pomegranate does not want to be cut, blackens my knife… Your hands are strong, nails sharp. Someday I will try to recall the sound of your fingers splitting the bright orange rind. You tear it apart like a wound…Violet blood squirts in our eyes, magenta flesh shimmers over battalions of seeds.

"My story? Okay," you say. "Evening falling, storm coming, I will oblige. I served in our army. Confined to barracks, we all bitched. I took leave. Clandestine, of course. 'You'll get shot,' my friends warned. 'Go to hell,' I said, and returned from town bearing shashlik and wine. While figuring how to slip in past the guard, I took a piss. Electrified wire was strung on my path. I might have died, but that flash lighted my way to the barracks. My brush with the Eternal was banal, obscene, and caused the death of another: the guard was electrocuted…How empty this bottle…. Waiter, more wine?

You, darling girl, wish to collect one more heroic epic? Here, to face life is heroic enough, to stay alive, avoid incidents, are the epics…Waiter! Cognac to warm us!"

The waiter warns the café must soon close. "Cognac? Two plum brandies. Turkish coffee? Baklava?"

"My cousin owns that blue house across the square. He's gone this week, left keys beneath the third flowerpot. Come along—we will be safe from the storm for the night."

"My bus leaves in two minutes!"

"Another ride through our mountains? Then don't be late for your next brush with death…We will meet in the capitol, or the hereafter." You kiss my hand, then embrace me, whisper: "No freedom here."

"I do know your history, read papers, books…" I proffer a tatter of napkin, my pen. "Please write down your name and address for me."

You crumple and toss the napkin, pocket the pen, scribble on the wind. "These, sweet girl, are my name, my address—"

Suddenly one long kiss. My bus stops. I give you the rest of the pomegranate. As I climb the steps, two guards seize my arms, help me into the bus, warn: "That man— danger!"

Other uniformed men chase after you through the square.

You filter quickly away through the crowd.

The driver jolts me aboard, speeds into the storm

***

The next day's newspaper reports: A man without a name is dead. Smudged passport shows no origin. His pockets bulged with poems in tongues no one can decipher. Blood level: *high*. Ironic smile. Cause of death still undetermined. The "bloodstains" mere pomegranate juice. No witnesses have come forth. Unless his kin are located, the morgue must file a blank report.

Bony footprints in the snow, frozen drops of noble blood, all disappear in storms that cover this black earth.

Through the rest of my life, I carry you inside as if the fetus of a royal child in fairy tales.

And as in old Slavic fairytales, every New Year's Morning you step from my looking glass, blow a kiss, then disappear.

Lotus Flower

Material: Recycled Copper
Size: 6-8" Diameter
Color: Brown, Green or Blue patinas
Can be used for indoor or outdoor display

The Red Pickup

RED PICKUPS hunted and haunted her. Red pickup trucks now were everywhere, with women drivers surely the pick-up kind, wearing animal fur and helmets of dyed blond hair; like that woman.

That fateful morning before Advent, however, Winifred must focus on the sermon she was mentally composing: *Is Good inevitably balanced by Evil in both Old and New Testaments, and likewise in contemporary life?* Years of Plenty were more than balanced by Years of Drought, so the situation was familiar to her parishioners.

Winifred had only nicked the rim above the rear tire of that woman's red pickup. Nothing to hinder its looks or functioning. Imperceptible except to whatever individual might take a chamois to the vehicle' flanks. In this case, an unlikely event.

The scrape was visible on Winifred's bottom-of-the-line bright green Hyundai. Long-dented but freshly shampooed, the car was a hand-me-down from Aunt Frances, who could no longer navigate country roads and had moved into a retirement home nearby, close enough to monitor her niece. "Drive carefully, dear. The good Lord and I will be watching."

The good Lord surely had more pressing matters on His plate, Winifred thought. Her car, however, would be easy for the good Lord and everyone else to watch: it glowed fluorescent green. She blessed the sartorial camouflage of her hard-won profession: black robes in church and occasionally out, otherwise her discreet gray skirt or brown slacks.

Not a profitable profession. Sunday's meager-as-ever take- in-the-plate, intended for bank deposit, consisted of several singles, dimes and quarters, which she slipped into her pocket, whence they further slipped through holes into the coat's lining. Just when parish bills for heating and electricity were highest, her flock couldn't tithe even five percent of whatever their earnings: everyone incurred extra expenses around holidays. Christmas Eve, parishioners might bring their contributions of Food for the Needy for Christmas, but it was *now*, one whole week before Christmas, that the Needy needed those dented cans of spaghetti, okra, Spam, items the donors were glad to clear from their cupboards.

Five black-walnut pies–this being the year the old tree beside the parish house bore walnuts—the church ladies proudly presented to Winifred. She thanked them sincerely, but she'd never mentioned her allergy to nuts, so she passed the walnut pies on to the Needy. *Pies for the P* oor echoed in her head like old English street cries or particularly insidious commercials. But the Needy would be grateful for any and all donations. So would she.

Winnifred would especially have relished the fruitcakes sprinkled with brandy, which the parish ladies brought to the Advent celebration. But the deacon tasted a slice and warned, "The good Lord would insist that no right-minded preacher should risk those brandy-saturated concoctions!" And saying that he had a bunch of relatives arriving tomorrow, he took the branded fruitcakes home himself.

Winifred's more important concerns today were automotive: her Hyundai supposedly had dented the red pickup which its driver had plunked where nobody could fail to collide: askew in the bank's jammed PARKING lot. The good Lord might have observed the incident, but had certainly been distracted by vaster collisions elsewhere in His world.

The curses cascading from that dyed-blonde pickup- driver had been ungodly. In Winifred's parish, although of course men knew all sorts of swear words, they curbed their language in a lady's presence.

No *lady* , that woman, and her language was unladylike.

She was swaddled in what Winifred, a lifetime member of Save-the-Animals: Banish-Fur-Coats, hoped was only *fake* rabbit fur, and the two teen-aged girls enveloped in—*fake* raccoon fur?—lolled against the pickup's fenders, arguing what they might get as compensation for Winifred's nicking of that unnecessary aluminum fender strip.

"Make her pay, Ma, real good!"

Given all the other dents and scrapes on the pickup's sides, with immense gentleness Winifred suggested their fender strip might have been dented already.

"Goddamit, my people'll get in touch with your people!" This sounded to Winifred like a line from a movie she had never watched. That woman was copying the Hyundai's license plate. Winifred couldn't act quickly enough to take the other party's particulars: no paper in pockets, purse or glove compartment...

After ripping more of her coat's lining, she extracted the parishioners' recent donations to the pass-around plate, destined for church repairs and utilities as well as the minister's meager salary. "Look, ma'am, all I have. Wouldn't cost thirty-six dollars for someone to smooth the nick..."

Anything to quiet her, keep her from reporting the "accident." Winifred dared not challenge her own precarious car insurance policy, nor mention that the thirty-six dollars were designated to pay the parish-house utilities.

As for police—no difficulties, please! The sheriff belonged to a rival parish but had made untoward advances toward Winifred. Troubles enough when her parishioners parked on the rows of kale at the farm next door. The farmer disparaged Winifred's defense of the starving rabbits nibbling his bountiful crops, and posted a *NO PARKING* sign in his garden.

That woman inspected the cash.

"With a rubber mallet or ball-peen hammer, ma'am," Winifred said, "you could smooth it yourself in a flash." Not that Winifred had ever pounded out a dent in a car, but with the parish claw hammer knew now to bang a nail in a wall. She did not herself know anyone with a ball-peen mallet, but someone around must have one.

The haranguing continued, decibels undiminished. The woman's potato face showed not gratitude but distrust. Six- foot-something tall and exceedingly well-fed, she looked fierce enough to take a mallet to Winifred.

Winifred knew that behind her back, people called her "Rev' Wee Weenie Winnie." True, she was short, the cuffs of her slacks had to be thrice rolled, her aunt's hand-me-down brown coat drooped: i.e., she looked bedraggled under a brown knitted cap, altogether anonymous. Granted how could a stranger know to show whatever respect was customarily given clergy of whatever denomination?

"One of your neighbors must be able to come up with a — softheaded hammer."

In Winifred's parish, *Love Thy Neighbor* was more than a biblical admonition. People helped each other. Nobody argued about payments there. On Loaves-and Fishes Saturdays, anglers (she was one) shared by-catch from the nearby lake.

Gardeners (she was not one) shared their extra tomatoes, zucchinis, rutabagas, winter kale. The choir's baritone, a mechanic by day, drove out nights to rescue neighbors with breakdowns. Although he looked with longing at Winifred as well as her Hyundai, he never touched bodywork. The local roofer—who also looked with longing—fixed parish leaks for two six-packs of cranberry juice.

Nothing to write on—Finally the Hyundai yielded one rumpled program of last Sunday's prayers and hymns someone had left in a pew, though on one side the margins were too narrow to scribble anything but the pickup's license plate number, not the woman's particulars. In the blanks on the reverse, in tidy penmanship some parishioner inattentive to hymns, prayers, or to Winifred's sermon, in careful cursive had written: *detergent, cantaloupe, strawberries, tomatoes, cukes, muffins, zebras, bread*— What are zebras?

At least That Woman did not belong to Winifred's parish. Her parish wasn't registered with a specific denomination, but embraced a cornucopia of godly philosophies espousing community and humanism. Along the county roads there were churches labeled *Abundant Harvest, Living Water, Tree of Life, Crossroads, Cornerstone, Healing and Deliverance, Oasis of Victory, Redemption, Whole Heart Deliverance, Fitley Joined Together*—and only the Lord knew what else. Her church, she liked to think, embraced them all.

As the lone female in her divinity-college class, she'd already encountered challenges enough from her male classmates, future shepherds-of-earthly-flocks. Some of them might uncharitably but possibly have maneuvered for Winifred to be assigned this distant rural parish "where she will do the most good."

Her loyal flock here enjoyed her interactive sermons on spiritual and secular issues, her mini-library, and especially the Coffee Hour to which the parish ladies' contributed their baked goods. The Health Department unpredictable about its visits to inspect premises serving food, Winifred was always swift to sweep up and scatter the crumbs for God's sparrows, the used coffee grounds to fertilize the flowerbeds, used paper plates for the wood stove, used Styrofoam cups into black plastic bags.

Those bulging bags today were squeezed inside the Hyundai for impending recycling at the county dump. She hoped the car had enough gasoline to get there and back: she must fill up very soon.

En route, red pickups tailed her on highways, across crossroads, parking lots, country roads.

That pickup had been a what? Dodge? Ford? Crusader?

She seldom noticed brands.

The gas gauge indicated EMPTY. Winifred pulled into the local WAWA.

"You could never miss that lime green car!" exclaimed the man at the next pump. "Seasonal for Christmas!" Agreeing about "unbelievable gas prices," Winifred inserted her credit card, filled and fled, turning down a lane between fields. She gathered handfuls of mud to smear over the Hyundai, covering the license plate. She was hungry, but, pausing outside the no-frills mini-market for oatmeal and milk, when a red pickup—whatever the brand—pulled in, she switched gears and headed to the nearby Dollar store for one can of chicken noodle soup on sale, then on to the county dump.

But spotting another red pickup at RECYCLING, she detoured a half-mile east to cheer up an ailing parishioner. She herself felt far from cheerful. Just before CLOSING HOUR she returned to the dump, tossed trash bags into the caboose which served as a bin, then drove home through the dark.

Cars following behind evidently felt she drove not quickly enough. Drivers honked, and passed her. She wasn't a fast driver: others drove too fast. When tailgated, she'd pull over on a shoulder. Now Winifred envisioned red pickups slowing, circling her Hyundai, halting and parking squarely ahead. The first pickup's rear window sported a decal: charging Mustangs. The second flaunted a Confederate flag. A pickup with a covered truck bed urged NEVER DRIVE TOPLESS. Did they all carry rifles under the seats? Pistols in open glove compartments? Chainsaws?

She maintained the perilous pace, repeating *Not paranoia, this is not paranoia* . She dared not confide in the deacon nor in any of her parishioners, she visited a doctor only for annual flu shots. She became aware of her lack of confidence and confidantes, and her unwanted apartness. She realized that even as a child she'd felt distant from her schoolmates. A perfect record of A's and Excellent Behavior had set a bell jar over her.

Someone pulled into the church parking lot. She recognized Deacon Evans' van with stickers proclaiming JESUS IS LORD. The deacon presented her with fresh pine boughs tied with a red ribbon around a bait-casting rod, the Santa tag reading "Happy Christmas from the congregation. Good catches come spring!" With a grand gesture, next he glued a bumper sticker reading FISHER OF SOLES on the Hyundai's dirty right flank. Although wary of ostentatious advertising, she thanked him and back in the parish house located a HONK IF YOU LOVE JESUS sticker to cover that nicked left flank.

The lake beyond the community dock froze over but nobody had ever bothered to chop a hole. She would now. With the claw hammer…Fish, alas, hibernated. So dinner seemed to be locked in destiny's cold storage…Her shelves grew bare.

Sundays' lower takes-in-the-plate lowered levels in mouse-proof jars protecting Winifred's flour, sugar, beans, bran flakes.

Another week before contributions were due to dribble in. Pursuit by shadowy pickups continued to dampen a season meant to be joyful. Prayer didn't help: red pickups skidded into her prayers as into her nightmares.

Parishioners meanwhile considered Winifred a role model, especially for the few young people who attended church, mainly for the Youth Socials always graced with donuts and cookies. She'd taught several of the parishes' teenagers to drive, and was relieved none of them owned dirty red pickups; they preferred shiny maroon coupes with fluorescent decals. Raising money washing cars, now they offered, "We'll scrub your Hyundai for Christmas; Granny says it looks 'disgraceful.' We'd even repaint it, put on skins with flames! Free!"

"Thanks…Bless you. But plain black paint, please."

The choir's conductor drove in. His wife's pink van was plastered with signs advertising *Catering, In- Home Pet Neutering, Astrological Readings.* He had laryngitis. Winifred was secretly relieved: he liked New Age hymns more than she did, and at every funeral belted out "Amazing Grace." She couldn't abide "Amazing Grace," and circulated prayers for the health of her parishioners. Her own throat raspy, she delivered abbreviated sermons admonishing pure thoughts, noble deeds, and old-fashioned English carols. It was beginning to snow but because the church's occasional janitor had gone to Minnesota for the holidays, after parishioners tracked it in, Winifred herself took the mop to the parish hall floor, and felt almost noble.

And her own fortunes improved: the farmer in the adjoining property plowed the snow from the church parking lot, the candle-shop donated its unsold if imperfect red tapers to the church, the Health Department inspectors arrived but as a blizzard was breaking, they quickly departed. A pigtailed child brought leftover fudge: "Please give these to The Baby Jesus, so now will I get Salvation?"

"Yes, dear."

Before realizing it, in her office Winifred (may the Baby Jesus forgive her) finished every sticky brown crumb—which would anyway have frozen solid en route to Heaven.

Coughing vigorously, the burly baritone-mechanic, a bachelor, brought her six poppy-seed pastries to show off his new baking, but warned that poppies and nutmeg were "reputedly hallucinogenic." Praying they did not contain his germs, she consumed every flesh-colored crumb.

Friday before Epiphany, snow masked her Hyundai as she inched toward the bank. Was the whole county depositing paychecks, covering debts, withdrawing money to create new debts? She parked to withdraw her last twenty. Behind, a red pickup stopped askew, positioned where anyone would hit it.

Winifred recognized the driver's helmet of brilliant blond, the rabbit-fur coat matching the pickup. That woman got out, slammed the truck door, and stomped unevenly into the bank.

Edging from the Hyundai, with one gloved finger Winifred brushed snow from the pickup's left rear fender, and discerned the loosened strip. Not hammered smooth by anyone. Surely that woman, deciding the nick wasn't that bad, had drunk Winifred's cash meant for a ball-peen hammer. The evidence was visible through the bank's picture window: that woman was wildly swinging her arms, pushing through lines, bumping a man with a cane, grazing an elderly lady, overturning a stroller, finally profusely kissing the bank officer, and shouting "Merry Christmas to all!"

Winifred could have made the excuse she herself was light-headed, having eaten only hallucinogenic poppy-seed pastry and double fudge, and though she was not generally a beer drinker, she had finished off a can of flat Red Bull discovered behind a drape after a Youth Social.

She could say that snow blinded her eyes, the Hyundai's mirrors, the pickup, her judgment. Could have said—

The surveillance camera lens focused only on the ATM machine. Might there be something to the Old Testament "eye-for-an-eye," though could any prophet have foreseen electronic eyes?

Back in the Hyundai, she turned the key, put the clutch into reverse, stepped on the gas pedal, backed, and enjoyed the clang and crunch.

Sunshine transformed ice-coated tree skeletons into shimmering sculptures. Winifred remembered the baritone had promised to leave a fruitcake on her doorstep, warning, "My fruitcakes are too strong for any Needy but—!" Her throat eased in anticipation. What those crumbs would do for God's sparrows! She pictured them flitting unsteadily through the crisp air, wobbling on the church eaves before sleeping off the brandied fragments of fruitcake...

She could even start looking back at the men who still studied her. She lowered a window as Vs of geese, like dark angels, honked low overhead, and she sped homeward singing "*Praise God From Whom All Feathers Flow.*"

Then, though she had no idea whence the words came or if there were a tune, she sang out, *Into Every Life A Little Sin Must Fall.*

Gaia
Material: Cold Cast Bronze
Size: 24H x 8W x 8D

Amanda

DRAT, no matter how slowly I pry the screen door, that falsetto click-click-click sounds out. This time, at least, it can't wake Mrs. Bromley: my hands—cramped, horrid—managed to dribble all my morphine into her strawberry milkshake. Drop by drop, one, two three, four, six—

Whose are those slender horses across our field? Foals of my old Palominos? I taught children, grandchildren, to ride on them. Blue ribbons, shiny under dust, still flutter above the stalls. Didn't I have to sell our horses? How did—

Deer. Big enough to saddle and bridle. When the farm was fenced, deer stayed in woods and fields. Fences broken, woods thinned, fields up the road manicured into lawns and "housing estates," deer take refuge here. Too early for oaks or apple trees to produce bounty for them, and though it's already August the vegetable garden lies fallow, so deer are trimming grass that someone, I forget his name, meant to mow. Anyway,

I prefer meadows to lawns, deer to noisy machines.

Careful with these old porch stairs! Hold both iron banisters… Rusted, must repaint—

Must keep my balance! Watch out that I don't talk to myself aloud: they say I do. But except for the occasional visiting grandchild, no one's left to talk with. Mrs. Bromley likes to talk, but is so set in her views! Maybe I am in mine…

Sorry, osprey, I didn't mean to scare you from your dead sycamore. At least your soprano peep-peep is too feeble to wake Mrs. Bromley, or distract the two brown thrashers cavorting like lovers in a dust puddle, or startle the great blue heron   stalking the shallows, each footstep deliberate, elegant.

How painful my inelegant knees. Each footstep stabs through

my feet. Dear Granny, forgive me that as a child I didn't pay enough homage to your aches.

Careful, a forgotten croquet ball—watch for wickets— No, a terrapin I almost tripped on. Football-size. Oh, hello, old girl. here's the "X" naughty grandson Noah carved on your dark-green shell. I'm sorry. You lumber ashore late this year.

Glad I stuck around through June, when except for laggards like you, by late May most turtles have clambered ashore to lay eggs. From the veranda I try to note where they're digging, so I can direct Noah where to find the leathery eggs for transfer to flower pots inside where raccoons can't get them.

Within weeks, can't remember how many, hatchlings are scrambling around inside the screened porch. The old turkey roaster full of dirt becomes their aquarium until we can escort the hatchlings to the river. Next June, Noah promises—

Poor Terrapin X, you're exhausted digging, but you've still got to make it to the shore, then paddle downriver while the tide— Wheelbarrow blocks your way! With my cane, I'll nudge you, like a ball, toward the river. We both have deliberate journeys ahead.

Is your duck blind still in the river, Judge Reilly? My eyes can't see that far.

What, all three cats? Oh, Snowball, I've got to brush your white angora fur. Left eye blue, right eye green, throwback to nobler ancestry…I left you cats at home, stretched on the windowsills, barely stirring to chase katydids. Now, you— Okay, come along, but don't trip me. Winter nights, you fellows warm me better than hot water bottles.

"You're a benevolent witch surrounded by familiars," Judge Reilly said as he watched me feed apple cores to the young raccoon while the bantam hen clucked around. Neither critter bothered the other. "No wonder you're named Amanda, Latin for She Who Must Be Loved." Or was it She Who Must Love?

Judge Reilly, my last love, now dead as the rest…At least we stayed uncaged, we outfoxed unfit spouses, officious social workers and neighbors who think everyone older should be incarcerated. They label my critters "another sign of unhealthy isolation—Ma'am, you should've moved, been moved, into our new state-of-the-art Home surrounded by well-kept lawns and folks your age. A trained staff. Not questionable women like Mrs. Bromley."

Bless you, Judge Reilly, for springing her from jail: Mrs.

B's braining her common-law spouse with a skillet was unquestioned self-defense. Three half-fried eggs, splattered along with her blood, proved evidence enough. I took her in, and now she looks after me, fetches groceries, helps me dress, pushes that blasted wheelchair. So willy-nilly I'm cared for, and she has a home…

But Mrs. B. chatters constantly, tidies so nobody can find anything, and feels uneasy out here: "Never know who'll pull down that long dirt road, or land on the shore, hide in them woods! A woman alone—" Nervous Nelly, checking the umbrella stand for intruders hiding among the old skates, baseball bats, walking sticks, relics from when the woods sported paths and the river froze.

They can't understand how, after an overpopulated life, I want *solitude* . People surrounded me even *in utero* : my fetal brain surely heard clamor around my ballooning mother. Older siblings Agatha, Horace, Hammond, the twins Edwina and Etta, all bossed me till they left the farm for jobs elsewhere. My sisters ended their lives slowly in retirement communities, my brothers quickly on highways….

Upon marriage, husband Burt took over the bossing, his bluster, sometimes violence, enough for six men.

I didn't boss Burt Jr. and Madeleine more than necessary. Dear Granny, you taught me to play the piano, I taught

Burtie and Madeleine. We sang, I read aloud *Wind in the*

Willows, Sea- Beach at Ebb Tide, and poetry to pupils, children, then to grandchildren. We tuned in Saturday operas and Sunday symphonies on the radio—I've read that fetuses absorb Mozart—though when Burt came in, he switched to hillbilly.

Still, Granny, our children came out all right: Madeleine played piano, if mostly show tunes, and Little Burtie Jr.'s trumpet even if it sounded like a wounded bull. What if fetuses hear only heavy metal?

Now Noah's like that heron: tall, thin, graying, solitary.

Joshua's more an osprey: plump, hunched, fierce glare, retreats with feeble arguments. And Sylvie, our wren too small to dance *Swan Lake,* forever rehearsing for when someone discovers her…Or was I the one practicing for elusive shreds of fame?

A sagging rainbow of colors dangles like a dead toucan: abandoned balloons. When your pony turned two, you festooned the barn with balloons till they spooked the horses. Winter afternoons inside snow forts, we ate hot buns, summers we caught perch, jumped off the pier, dodged the jellyfish, and at night kicked up fireworks of luminescence in the river…the river where I'm heading, turtle-speed…

I know each birthday is expected to be my last. Ninety, ninety-one, ninety-two, was the last ninety-seven? Have I fooled everyone, if not myself, hanging around like those drooping balloons dancing in the wind…

Remember those generations I taught at the schoolhouse? If parents were ill or fighting, I boarded their children. Rescued mothers from abusive husbands, tended their bruises, tended my own. As one old bruise fades, another purples this epidermis thin as onionskin. Mrs. B calls my long-sleeved blouses I wear to hide them a disgrace. "Rags! What if someone sees you?"

But visitors only appear by mistake. Or like that persistent minister who comes by to determine if I've made my peace with God.

"God is my gardener, I let Him do his job in peace. We both let the farm follow its own designs. While it could use human intervention, I don't need anyone to intercede between God and myself."

How the minister twitched when wrens swooped through an unscreened window to their nest on the mantel! "Closest I have to angels," I said. Then a leopard frog jumped onto his shoulder. "Frog's just chasing mosquitoes," I explained.

When the frog landed on his knee, he leapt up. "My wife's waiting—" His sweet wife, cowering like a mouse under his disapproving eyes.

I never asked those brow-beaten wives: "Why stay married?" True, I myself couldn't have left you, Burt, since on the eve of our marriage, you asked for our failing family farm as a dowry. Grandmother disapproved of your planting tobacco and smoking—"tobacco leaches the lungs as well as the soil"— but it grows well and the homestead stayed in the family.

Tobacco is now a crop of the past though it's what made gentlemen farmers prosper. But something's always out to kill us.

What of our promised honeymoon in Paris? Instead you bought the pack of hounds so you could "ride like a proper gentleman." I didn't argue. A bride at seventeen, in teacher's college...

But I began agriculture courses-by-mail, farmed, bore two babies, taught, saved, one July took Burtie Jr. and Madeleine to France. During our absence, you rode my mare too hard, ruined her forelegs, shot her "mercifully."

Then, arguing for better cash crops than corn or soybeans, you planted tobacco again. Shuffling in the bedroom ceilings might be raccoons, but knockings on walls, when no trees grew close enough to hit, could only be angry ghosts...

We planted winter wheat, and noises diminished. Pots, plates and paintings still fell on their own whenever you flew into your rages...

Granny again visits my dreams. Mother and Father too. Sometimes Etta, Horace, Hammond and Agatha—and what were those other names? Their visits aren't scary, everyone's laughing and talking. Welcoming?

But Granny, it was Burt, not I, who moved you and Father and Mother to the "The Wrinkle Factory," the ramshackle Institution for the Elderly, though most neighbors were living and dying at home.

You're all long in the cemetery. Burt, not long enough.

Granny, you can return whenever you want. Madeleine's away now, remember, she died of leukemia. Her distraught young husband—what was his name?—joined the Merchant Marine but sent Little Sylvie dolls from distant ports long after she'd outgrown toys. Burtie Jr. died in an accident in an Army jeep after his wife took up with a horny colonel.

Now they all call me "Gramanda." Natural they'd leave the farm for college and jobs, but holidays draw them back. "Oh, Gramanda! Another litter of kittens under your bed!" And: "Look, a black snake in the wisteria!"

"Cats and snakes, they'll all settle our mice, dear."

Would I could move as swiftly as cats, snakes or mice. Yet today, however slowly, I am slipping away from Mrs. B.'s watchful eyes… As I used to from Burt's parties, with their loose ends of chatter, music, smells of spilled beer and grilled deer wafting after them. The men complimented me warmly on my apple cakes and same old blue dress, but under Burt's watchful eye, they didn't hover long. Intimidated by my schoolmarm reputation, the wives complimented me on my salads and cakes, averting their eyes from my same blue dress, rather low cut. But if we went for a walk, Burt trailed us, his hawking and coughing preceding him. "Why in hell you sneaking off, woman? You meeting someone in the woods?"

Though I'd not planned to meet anyone, Burt, you accused me, cursed me, swung so hard that my face was bruised purple.

Yet Father, your words, as when I complained of siblings teasing me, echo still: *Don't play the victim, darling. Work to become stronger and brighter than everyone else.* Not so simple, Father, but I've repeated your advice to Madeleine and Burt Jr., later to Noah, Joshua and Sylvie, and to hundreds of pupils.

Only after you'd all gone your ways, did I sneak off to meet anyone.

Sad, to outlive lovers…

My caregivers are instructed, "Keep watch, the old gal thinks she can still walk to the mailbox or sail." Finally deeming me incapable of navigation beyond the veranda, Mrs. Bromley relaxes.

Took my magnifying glass to decipher the tiny print: *Each mL of Roxanol TM contains: Morphine Sulphate 20 mg.* My darn eyes gave out before I could unravel the warnings.

Strawberry milkshakes, however, mask additives. So Mrs. B. is collapsed like an empty sail bag or spent balloon, she'll sleep like the supposedly dead, though dead don't snore like chain saws.

The morality of my actions doesn't trouble me: when they thought me asleep, I've watched Mrs. Bromley and fill-in caregivers filching my medications. One drop-in nurse transferred my morphine to her nasal spray bottle, then when I observed her sniffing it, protested, "Anyone would catch cold in this drafty old house, Ma'am."

Is morphine easier on the gastrointestinal track if inhaled?

So you can turn soap operas high?

"At that modrun convalescent home where I normally work," one fill-in nurse insisted, "we're taught television keeps even comatose patients from feeling isolated."

"I prefer isolation, and I'm not yet comatose. Please turn that blasted thing off."

My sewing scissors finally managed to close on the electric cord. Someone replaced it, and since then I can't locate any scissors. "Disappeared" in case I take it into my head—?

Today, pains undiminished but head clear thanks to my holiday from medications, however ungainly my gait, I wobble from tree to tree...

How many saplings have sprung up on the lawn! An orchard now! Crabapple saplings, then hawthorns, crepe myrtles, spindly maples, apple trees, finally pines. Around the perimeter, long-standing cedars and oaks: pin-, water-, and willow oaks. I keep mental lists of trees the way Burt memorized his sizes of bolts and nails, screws, wires, pipes.

The cats wander off: mole here, striped skink there. Oh, my heart's pounding, like winter waves against the pier! Let's rest a moment—Locate the Adirondack chairs…A flash of a white tail by the berry patch—I'll sit—What, and risk not being able to pull myself up again? As Burt would say, *Hey- ell, no!*

Another white tail of a buck vaulting into the briars, his half-snort, half-sneeze sounded like Burt when he came.

Drat! I'm wearing not slacks or a skirt, but a bathrobe!

And silly slipper-socks! No wonder the pebbles and sticks hurt my feet. Mrs. Bromley, you forgot to dress me! Assumed I'd return to bed after lunch, so why bother? Heavens, I'm not bedridden yet! You stuff me into a chair to confront some tasteless pureed mess–Cain killed Abel over porridge like this? At least mealtime my wrists aren't tied to bedrails.

At least this bathrobe has pockets. And you didn't check them… What a tangle of thorns! Brambles snatch me, scratch! If I fell, could I get up? What stupidity, forgetting the berry patch! Last month you–no—last year—Mrs. B, you're too portly— a grandchild, Noah? Joshua? Sylvie?—wheeled the chair while I filled the colander with ripe blackberries.

"But persons your age," Mrs. Bromley warned, "should avoid raw fruit, especially what don't come packaged from supermarkets."

"Nonsense. Not my stomach dying, just bones." Damn the et cetera. I swallowed the berries whole, the only ill effects my inky clothes. Unfashionable anyway.

And wasn't that clever, how in a rare private moment, I stuffed the last berries into Burt's silver flask along with a tablespoon of sugar, and filled the remaining space with vodka! More palatable than morphine. Also more organic: Noah would approve. What was it he studied? Botany? Or was that Joshua?

The flask is now in my bathrobe pocket.

Crows! Hush! Your alarms could wake the dead, or the drugged. Please don't caw any louder! And Osprey on your dead sycamore, stay silent. Nothing perturbs you, Heron? So slender and stately, your head high, dive for a minnow, then— Goodness, you've speared a young eel! What a tussle! Finally you wangle one end into your beak, raise your head so it slips down your gullet—the way sips of vodka trickle down mine.

I'm dizzy. They say I'm losing a half-pound a week.

Tonight, Mrs. B, we'll have fish for supper: I'll drop a line off the pier for catfish, big whiskered monsters. Carrots from—

From the garden now absorbed by forest. Last hurricane tore planks from the pier. Noah promises—

Did I forget my itinerary? Onward! *Right foot, left foot,* what Grandfather said soldiers marched to in the Civil War,

Hay foot, straw foot, belly full of bean soup. That's how I taught my pupils right from left. Giant Steps—

Ouch! Help! Lost my balance! I've fallen into the underbrush! Pain spears my left shoulder, might be broken. Same shoulder shattered at age ten, falling off a horse leaping a jump—

Again I'm cushioned, pin-cushioned, by blackberry thorns. A fakir's bed of nails.

The flask's blessedly intact...

Sun burns through the leaves. Oh, dear: poison ivy. A mean joke, to die imprisoned by thorns and breaking into rashes! An ugly corpse I'd make, scratched, blistered and bloated. If no one found me until winter when foliage dies, I'd still resemble that deer skeleton in the marsh. Aesthetically preferable, but not how I envisioned my vaunted end-of-life solitude.

Madeleine imagined her own body "like the pallid innards of the last watermelon in the garden, the one we should have left." Dear Madeleine, you loved metaphors. I recall "O Captain, my captain, our fearful trip—"

"And with poetry," Madeleine said, "I can devour much more in a short time." Foreseeing you'd have only a short time? I preferred novels in those minutes when I wasn't studying about crops or some newfangled thresher Burt brought home to test but he refused to read directions, claimed he just *knew.* So back to REPAIRS...

They say poetry heals, but…Earlier, I wouldn't have dreamed of dying alone. After all the crowded occasions of others' passings, that claptrap of bedside vigils, long faces, faked smiles and forced tears, all those congenital or do I mean congenial rituals in which one participates. Some tears were real indeed…

How brittle are—stiffs. As a child, seeing grandfather laid out, I asked, "If he could stayed soft, would he keep alive? Or rot?"

Your funeral, Burt, comes to mind. More dignified than you deserved, but I kept up the farce. Including about your demise, officially from "coronary thrombosis." You yourself then downed all those peculiar pills at once with Jim Beam, you sent me out to feed your yapping hounds. In books, dying masters' dogs howl. When you expired, no hound howled. Nor did the dogs complain when I parceled them out among your old buddies, on condition nobody bring them back to chase my critters.

Several of those old buddies kept showing up, offering help around the farm: *Such a pretty widow, isn't she lonely?*

She is not, thanks. She drives the tractor herself. Corn, wheat and soybeans grow green as ever. Did I become captain of my own ship?

Oh, Burt, how people smiled at that huge granite stone you'd ordered with bas-reliefs of hounds! "Blessed hounds of heaven," the old minister said, wryly. Rather, hounds of hell. Carved beneath your name: *and his wife Amanda.* Only these dates need chiseling in.

I will escape lying beside you for eternity, listening to your cough even in your coffin.

I must get up! But when I stay still, it hurts less.

At your wake, I learned of your last deal: selling our fields across the road to a developers. Dammit…True, some of that money helped the grandchildren through college. After your funeral expenses.

"Fireworks, firewater, all the venison a body could eat," your buddies kept recounting. "The old fart's wake is a blast!"

And a blessing. So might mine be, even absent a body to bless.

That real estate agent nosing around urged Mrs. B to phone

Goodwill "to fetch the sagging beds, stained sofas, split sheets, tattered towels, dented cauldrons, tone-deaf piano, do this quick before her heirs show the place."

Granny, I've other plans than let developers loose here, lucrative though this might be. A decade ago, Motor Vehicles wouldn't renew my license, but still I drove the battered tractor into the village, now town. Bob Reilly, that bright young lawyer unaware his grandfather was more than "just a family friend," he notarized my will designating the land as a wildlife preserve, the house a shelter for battered women. Those dusty canning cauldrons could feed thirty hungry souls. Piano and furniture are repairable. The cats are provided for with sacks of Kibbles which they guard against mice. My "immediate survivors" already enjoy their shares of cash that, little by little, I've withdrawn from the bank to spare them meddling accountants. Let my leftovers jumpstart their lives.

Granny, you'd approve of that young lawyer, Bob, who always come around whenever Sylvie visits. Now they are grown, do they think I don't know he sneaks into her bedroom on weekends? He looks like his granddad, younger.

My beloved Judge Reilly, you too would approve. You insisted long ago I burn your letters. To Mrs. B's consternation, charred bits still litter the kitchen. And ashes, like those I'd become if I listened to those people advocating cremation.

Ouch! Does anyone advocate death by berry barbs and poison ivy? Fire is cleaner.

Selfish to hang on so long…This morning Madeleine waved from the vegetable garden. Naturally a dream, no lettuce left by July. No Madeleine.

No more time to mourn those departed, or stick around to see how the living turn out. I've overheard the prognostications: first, "a year, at best," then "a month," now they whisper, "just a few days more…"

I've tried to follow Father's advice to "seize the day." Despite old responsibilities, now my darned infirmities, I have lived every day to the brim. Pain reassures: I am alive. Seize this hour—As if these cramped hands could seize anything.

Can't remain splat in the brambles. Did I hear the screen door creak? Cats! Sensing my dilemma, you followed, cluster on my chest, hot in this heat. Stop licking my face! You, Snowball, especially visible, might betray—Go home! Scat! Move!

I can't move. Must move, stretch my better hand, grab that thick vine. Leaves glisten poison. Terribly slowly, muscle by bone, pull myself up....Cradle the hurt arm, it outweighs old pains. At last! I can resume my crazy pace. You cats! Mrs. Bromley knows you always follow me—

Pity the dinghy is beached high above the tide line. I'd drag it to the water, push off as if to meet you, my beloved Judge...How many sunsets I've sailed or poled to your duck blind on stilts, trailing lines so my excursions appeared purposeful, Or you rowed ashore...Autumns and winters, strings of decoys floated from the blind. We never shot a bird. An hour or several, languid on faded quilts.

Perch or bluefish did indeed bite: we'd scale and gut them, cook on your Coleman stove or a campfire. We tonged the waters below the pilings, feasted on oysters and each other. You called me your "Venus on a half-shell."

Last night you visited my dreams. Said something about a boat. That dinghy still there! On closer inspection: eelgrass spikes through the hull, wasps unfurl from under the bow, mice have tatted the sails into lace.

I'm a shipless, shiftless captain now. Can't take any cat to sea in this pea-green boat. Even without an owl.

Early for owls. Yet last night a pair who-who-whoed back and forth for an hour. Scared the daylights out of Mrs. B.

The riverbank is steep. I know where muskrat and otter hide their dens, how after hurricanes, they burrow elsewhere.

Off shore, flotillas of turtles thrust periscopes above greenish brown ripples. Minnows school, crabs patrol. In deeper water, blue-fish. So even leaving, I'll have critters, my "familiars."

Dear dead Judge. We loved enough times to curl Snowball's fur, or that minister's bald head...To die while making love! Rather, after.

Who will brush you now, my cats? But stop hovering!

Darn stick-tights...Or am I the stick-tight?

I remember: it's Noah who studied ecology, will run the refuge. Joshua's degree agriculture, he'll farm. And Sylvie, a social worker, trained to run shelters. Mrs. Bromley can fuss over everyone, or not...So I can disengage myself with serenity.

Too perfect. Suddenly I want to stick around to see how it all turns out. Like losing a good book before you've finished it. I'll resume my morphine, concoct cocktails of Percodan and Oxycontin, let my zombied mind wander like that albatross—

Then what, sleep my way to death? Hey-ell no!

"Lord help us!" Back at the house, Mrs. B. is howling. Lord help us indeed: I did not drop enough drops of Roxanol in her milkshake. That woman will waddle like a huge snapper into the yard. Or up the drive, her charge escaped before—I overhear her shouting, "The old gal might fall—Break everything—How could she have fled wheelchair, house, yard, crawled the entire way to the road? Cars might strike her, someone might rob, kidnap, demand ransom—Sun setting already, Lord, help, we'll have to phone 911, launch a search—"

You remember, Judge, how Mrs. B. dislikes dealings with the law.

As Burt said, after a stag wandered into his sights that off- season evening and policemen started nosing around the swamp, "No way those motherfuckers gonna find any carcass around here. *Hey-ell no!*"

The late afternoon breeze is chilly for August. Yes, cold nights I am glad for you cats.

The water will be warm. Damn, I can't bend to test it, or pull off these ridiculous slipper-socks! Useless against oyster shells underfoot, jellyfish, crabs. I'll float above...Scratches bleeding too much, blood attracts sharks, they've been known to swim way upriver...

First, blackberry vodka …Wriggle it and me free of this blasted bathrobe. Venus again naked on her oyster shells—I'm laughing before the first sip!

Hey-ell, yes, down the vodka…Ouch! Slid down the bank.

How clumsy…

What silky water…What strange joy! Minnows kiss my thighs silver. Perch—Bluefish—

Beyond the river, out in the bay, beyond that, in the ocean, I'll nourish the fish that long nourished me.

Leviathan
Material: Resin, aqua finish
Size: 9H x 8W x 18L

His Painting Not on the Wall

THE WOMAN stretches nude in the window, her hands on the frame. From the log house, an unseen lantern illuminates her as she seems to watch the bony brown cow nuzzle invisible weeds in the dark farmyard.

Caught in the flow of light through the door, the man washes his head in a wooden bucket. Will she take him to bed, or stuff red peppers with onions and rice for his supper? First she must tend to the cow...

Now milk glows in the bucket. She feeds the cow grain she has saved. A black tree captures the red sun in a tangle of branches black against the purple-brown sky.

Reduced to essentials, no glass to protect the painting six decades old, landscape and figures forever are caught on a rectangle of cardboard he rescued from someone's trash outside his walk-up.

The grace of an invisible hard-bargain God glows through the painting, albeit the artist was not a believer, merely nostalgic for his distant dangerous land either way he risked leaving or staying.

Taking her own risks, every few days the lady managed to slip away from her house to visit him. She absorbed his brilliance, tenderness, ironies, daring, and left casseroles, sable- tipped brushes and new jars of paints outside his unanswered door: he might be away, or damn it, holed up inside with some other woman. Others loved him and he loved them back, but surely none loved him and risked as much as she did.

He had to return to his distant land. He took the sable brushes, but he left her the half-used jars of paint, blank and half-finished canvases, and his paintings.

She studied the blanks...

He inspired her own first paintings, though she only told him decades later when they met in his land across ocean and seas...

Their trysts, early and later, were never revealed, never betrayed.

When, another decade later, she read that in his village across the ocean he had just died, she dared not weep, nor mention his passing. At last she set to work on her own half-finished canvases stacked by the wall, and began to work on the blank ones...

In time she found the courage to enter exhibits, in time her paintings sold.

One rainy day still more decades later, hunched in the attic, she discovered passionate letters written to her by different, later, lovers... For others had loved her and she accepted whatever shreds of affection, but none did she love as she loved the dangerous artist.

Why do people yearn, she thought, beyond what they have inside their own lives...

This tale, decades old, is untold and, like other fables and fairy tales, invented and soon forgotten. But once you love someone, you love forever.

The Murder
Material: Mixed Media
Size: 10H x 24W x 12D

The Crawl Space

"MERELY THE SKIN of a black rat-catcher, Mr. Melton. No copper-head. And by August, all snakes are long gone from the cellar to the garden."

"I don't trust no snake nowhere," he said.

Generations of Meltons had been farmers and caretakers here, and this final descendant should be as accustomed to wildlife, even when not shooting it, Belinda Smithington thought as she knelt on wet grass outside the dark two-foot square opening beneath what the local paper used to call "Congressman Smithington's historic mansion." For years the scene of much partying and politicking, the structure was now only a ramshackle farmhouse no longer of interest to the press.

Snakes didn't spook Belinda. Granted benevolent black snakes squeezed their prey to death and could, if frightened, chomp on an ankle.

Congressman Smithington's mansion and its denizens were familiar to Belinda and to her cousin Daniel since childhood. Parlor and dining room were reserved for weekend politicking and partying, while various cousins from around the county entertained each other in the attic or the barn, accommodating Daniel's infirmities without question.

Plumbing beneath the house, however, remained mysterious, foreboding. Brushing aside cobwebs and dangling wires, she commandoed it into the crawl space.

"You okay going in there?" Daniel called from his wheelchair under the oak.

"Sure. Stay where you are!"

The crawl space was a labyrinth of grungy pipes, even dirtier than the cellar in the Gaza desert...Beneath the first floor, multiple pipes transported well water inside, other pipes carried wash water and sewage to a cesspool somewhere under the neglected gardens. A century of cinders, cement crumbs, insect carapaces, and good country dirt encrusted all.

Worried that Daniel might try to maneuver his wheelchair between the ruts, and tip over, she was relieved when Mr. Melton figured out which was the broken pipe, and she could exit, ripping her ragged jeans still more on nails.

Melton's forbearers knew in their bones which pipes went where, their lives successions of squats, kneels, wriggles and crawls, loosenings and tightenings, armed with wrenches, heavy-duty extension cords and flashlights.

Figuratively, Belinda's life was, she mused, and sometimes literally, a succession of squats, kneels, wriggles, crawls, loosenings, tightenings, armed with uncertain intellectual tools...

Clothes already torn beyond any hippie fashionableness would end up in the DONATIONS bag destined for anonymous Third World women to braid into colorful rugs, thanks to programs which, in air-conditioned offices, Belinda had helped create in lands which had seldom bothered with indoor plumbing before colonials felt the need...

In addition to help when abroad, in the mansion as in the long-ago apartment or house in Georgetown, the Smithingtons employed a chauffeur and a cook-housekeeper. A Missus Brown, born with Smithington genes "if diluted by cross-breeding," ruled the house and kitchen. During the week Mister Brown, handyman/butler/chauffeur, had ferried Congressman Smithington in the Caddy to his office in the Congressional building, and Melanie to various charity boards and other "activities which might prove politically useful." Missus Brown drove the children too and from elementary school in the old station wagon where Daniel's wheelchair could be folded into the rear.

"Guess while I was overseas," Belinda said to Mr. Melton, "the real estate agents handling tenants set up periodic pest-control visits?"

"And I and my father," Mr. Melton said, "we repaired the roof so no critters in the attic. Ouch, I'm gettin' old, stiff limbs. Sixty's time to retire."

Retire, only sixty? Belinda never revealed her age, except when essential on official documents. Her father had set the example: until his mid-eighties Congressman Smithington, who was also Daniel's adoptive father, continued running for office and getting elected, only retiring when Melanie Smithington tactfully brought up his increasing forgetfulness. He still made appearance at fairs, bull roasts, tractor pulls, graduations, parishes, and veterans' clubs.

Mingling with county gentry was especially important as he'd married Melanie, daughter of a minor foreign diplomat. Her British accent added class in Washington, balancing the congressman's folksy demeanor, but was "downright off-putting to some country folks." The local obstetrician who'd yanked Belinda from Melanie Smithington's womb sixty years ago had barely understood her Oxbridge accent.

The year before Belinda's birth, a few farms away, a baby was delivered of a mother born a Smithington but rather unfortunately married to an alcoholic fiddler named Hayes of not verifiable genealogy. Their baby Daniel was handsome and relatively undemanding, but Hayes suddenly noticed what others already had: legs uneven and twisted, the child at age four only crawled.

"A cripple!" Hayes exclaimed. "You must take him to see the doctor immediately!"

The doctor, whom mother and baby already visited for periodic check-ups, explained, "A few cases of infantile paralysis still appear in this country…"

To distract him during the examination, the pediatric nurse sang. Daniel sang back in perfect pitch. "Musically talented!" doctor and nurse exclaimed simultaneously.

Hayes was proud of his own musical talents but, realizing he'd sired an "imperfect" child, he drank ever more, more frequently landed in the county jail. The Salvation Army dried him out and steered him into the Merchant Marine, but when his ship docked in Venice, he vanished.

Daniel's mother died when their old tractor overturned.

His elderly grandmothers both lived on farms rife with ruts and crumbling structures "unsafe for the handicapped." The grandmother with a telephone dialed the congressman. "The child has our Smithington blood, and Daniel's your middle name...Belinda shouldn't grow up a spoiled only child."

Melanie Smithington had agreed. Daniel was legally adopted. He seemed born musically talented, so Melanie nabbed an upright piano at the local thrift shop. Though Belinda proved to be tone deaf, she learned to read music and turn the pages of Daniel's scores.

Again Melanie Smithington agreed when the congressman insisted, "The children need a dog, a hunting dog, and I'll resume hunting as soon as the current 'Save-the-Wildlife' fad is over." He selected a grizzled Labrador called Butch from a neighboring farm.

A couple of years later, lacking the heart to consign the arthritic old dog to the vet's to be "put down," Butch died in the crawl space under the house. Beyond the gardens, one of the Meltons dug a grave deep enough to keep foxes from digging into it.

Seven-year-old Daniel crying inconsolably all night Belinda, then age six, held him, rubbing his twisted limbs. The next day she wheeled him up the dirt lane to the farm which produced dynasties of Labradors. Though Daniel swore nothing could replace Butch, Butch Junior curled up between the children, all three sleeping too soundly to be diverted by the thunderstorm and usual power failure.

"How sweet..." Belinda's mother murmured when she looked into Daniel's room, her candle flame making ghosts dance across the flowered wallpaper. She fetched her husband. "Come see our Heavenly Twins, and their new puppy—"

"Yep, honey, they're curled up like blacksnakes," the Congressman said. "And where blacksnakes live, aren't no copperheads. The way we Smithingtons want it: keep down undesirables in our county.

*

Age eight and the facts-of-life still hazy, Belinda worried less about the Congressman's inherent prejudices than the possibility that merely curling up with Daniel, she might become pregnant.

"My last routine radiologist appointment," he assured her, "the nurses were whispering about how 'repeated X-rays could cause sterility down the pike,' but when they realized I was listening, quickly said 'Oh Danny boy, you are too young to be concerned with such matters.' Back home, I opened the big dictionary."

*

Melanie remarked that "Local twang is dangerously contagious! We must import a proper English governess to cure the children's drawl and the absence of *g*'s on the ends of their gerunds. And they might finally acquire proper manners a well as accents."

A proper English governess was imported. One chilly bedtime, Daniel, Belinda and the Labrador curled up together, the governess entered to bring them each a quilt. "Heavens! You children are too old and your dog too doggy to be sharing one bed! What would people think!" Thereafter, they waited until the governess retired to her own room. Soon they convinced Melanie that, as they had overheard a teacher say, "Governesses are mighty elitist for a county congressman's kids."

*

The local schools had programs for blind and for deaf children but as yet none for the physically challenged. "We must take them into Washington with us," Melanie said, "and enroll them in a good private school!"

The Smithingtons moved to Georgetown, the large brick house and walled garden suitable for official entertaining as well as children and dogs. The house remodeled so Daniel would not have to navigate stairs, the servants' quarters off the kitchen became the children's bedrooms with playroom and bathroom between. The servants enjoyed the best views from their attic.

Belinda was allowed to sit in on Daniel's music lessons and he at her history classes. Though she could never master his scores, he memorized her assignments in French and international affairs.

Upon her graduation from school, on her teachers' advice, Belinda was sent to a women's junior college in New England. She was finally allowed to leave when the guidance counselor agreed she had become morose, anorexic and was obviously not benefiting from their fine studies program. Transferred to Georgetown University, she again lived at home with her parents and Daniel, regained her normal cheerful self, and both children maxed their respective exams.

The mansion in the countryside remained as it had always been, serving as an elegant weekend retreat, and Congressman and Mrs. Smithington continued to live there part of the time until a retirement home was built in the county.

For years Daniel avoided mentioning his handicaps until, reading one of Belinda's books from a literature course, he came across George Herbert. "Listen to this!" he said bitterly.

> *Man is all symmetry,*
> *Full of proportions, one limb to another,*
> *And all to all the world besides;*
> *Each part may call the furthest brother,*
> *For head with foot hath private amity*
> *which makes him pale and wan.*

Belinda had forgotten his anger at his condition. He regained composure only when she took up the book:

> *"The stars have us to bed;*
> *Night draws the curtain, which the sun withdraws;*
> *Music and light attend our head;*
> *All things unto our flesh are kind*
> *In their descent and being; to our mind*
> *In their ascent and cause."*

He shut the anthology, wheeled over to the windows, closed the curtains, and hauled himself from his wheelchair into his bed. She followed, and drew him close.

*

At seventeen, encountering Washington's perennial bright young interns and congressional aides, Belinda whirled through parties and balls. Considered "attractive rather than conventionally pretty," long black dresses at least made her look almost svelte.

Daniel wearing a tuxedo, in his wheelchair parked against a wall, people paused to exchange a few words, but he soon found their well-meaning condescension too galling. His musical studies increasingly serious, he gave them priority. One car adapted to his needs, he soon passed the driving test and drove himself to amateur classical orchestras and jazz bands. He began working paying gigs, playing light classics for weddings and bar mitzvahs, and tinkly cocktail music at piano bars. His infirmities merely drew larger tips. "Better than freeloading one hundred percent off relatives," he muttered, back in the kitchen thrusting a wad of twenties in the cookie jar. While waiting until Belinda came home, he'd listen to the university lectures she recorded: if never himself to join the State Department, he'd still learn everything she did.

Belinda's escorts were disappointed she gave them only a quick kiss on the doorstep, then hurried into the kitchen for cocoa with a dash of rum with Daniel, who would quiz her about some point in history.

*

Belinda did linger on the front stoop with one young law clerk. Boswell Bostwick, as his cumbersome name went, was a Bostonian with a 40-foot sloop and a future in the financial community. When he invited her on a sailing house party off Marblehead, Melanie paid for Belinda's ticket on the New Englander from Union Station. "Daniel could not easily manage leaping off trains and onto yachts— "Anyway, no invitation for him was extended.

Nor could Daniel have managed the duties of an usher when, four months later, in a chapel of the National Cathedral, Belinda was married to Boswell Bostwick. Daniel turned down their invitation to play Mendelson's Wedding March. "Too corny."

Belinda and Bostwick settled in his house in Boston. "I don't want a working wife," he insisted, so she took advanced political science courses at Radcliffe. She grew accustomed to his various yacht races and to his impulsive decisions, unexplained absences, and annoyance at her inquiries.

Their marriage proved childless and rather brief.

One rare weekend, instead of sailing off Cape Cod or skiing in the White Mountains, the young couple drove south in Bostwick's red Cadillac convertible "to check out your ancestral home." Bostwick found a half-drunk can of beer in the sink but when he poured out the dregs, the puddle remained. Belinda had little experience with plumbing matters, nor had Bostwick, but, he insisted, "I can fix any old kitchen sink as easily as the head on my yacht. Pipes probably clogged with roots from your damned overgrown fig bushes around the house."

He hunted in vain for a snaking machine, then drove off toward the local hardware store. When by morning he did not return, an earlier "Mr. Melton" reamed the drain clear.

Finally, Bostwick called from some telephone in what from the background noise sounded like a bar: "Hey, good weather ahead, I'm off sailing for a while, and—" When the operator interrupted for Bostwick to deposit more coins, he hung up. Belinda assumed he was just off for another race and would return in a few days. After a week in the old mansion, she dusted off one of the pickups in the barn and drove it to their Boston apartment. Another fortnight later, going through the mail, she finally opened his bank statements. These included restaurant bills for dinners to which she'd not been invited, department stores bills for lacy lingerie she never saw. When the mailman left a seemingly frantic love letter on pink notepaper from an unfamiliar female, she realized the situation. Daniel in the course of their near-daily phone conversations, suggested, "Perhaps under another name he flew with whatever sweetie to Paris—"

A week later, police knocked on the door to query Belinda about a red sports car abandoned in a seaside town: her name as well as

Bostwick's appeared on documents in the glove compartment. Then a dozen miles off New Jersey, the Coast Guard fished up the body of a man fitting Bostwick's physical description. Apparently fallen overboard, his ID had survived in the shorts pocket on the shark-nipped body. His yacht remained moored in another harbor, barnacles thickening on the cracks in the anti-fouling paint. The police distracted by other demands, the Smithingtons chose to avoid further investigations, especially during the congressman's election campaigns which kept him in the mansion.

Formalities over, Belinda accepted the status of early widowhood, resumed her maiden name, sold the yacht to pay Bostwick's debts, and did not pursue the mystery. Glad to be back with Daniel and occasionally her parents in the Georgetown house, she passed the Foreign Service exam and began her career at the State Department. Daniel continued his musical studies, played gigs around Washington and the adjacent counties, in between reading all her books, vicariously preparing for the diplomatic life.

Whenever a new post abroad needed a replacement in a hurry, she was a safe bet to fly over. A handicapped but mobile and intelligent adult dependent seemed easier to accommodate than children to enroll in local international schools or to send home at government expense. They had no trouble finding tenants for the Georgetown house.

Belinda performed her assignments quietly and her colleagues seemed unaware of or too polite to mention the unsolved mystery of her unfortunate marriage. Elegantly but conservatively groomed, a pleasant but not an undiplomatically merry widow, over time she developed the same chunky body as certain did other mid-life women in government careers. Colleagues liked her, and were impressed with Daniel's knowledge of international affairs as well as his musical talents. He read *The New York Times*, whether the specially delivered overseas edition or, eventually, online. He also perused whatever local papers, and seemed to know as much as Belinda of international affairs and indigenous customs. He continued his own career as a musician: He played whatever tuned-up piano in whatever American embassy, join local orchestras and bands, took on students, and provided windows into local worlds to which Foreign Service officers might not be invited but in which they often were interested.

In whatever locale, while ostensibly sleeping in their respective rooms, they curled up together in his bed.

*

On a special assignment to a certain country with which relations were minimal, they were forbidden to contact the few other Americans in the country. Ostensibly there as visiting teachers on a special exchange program, under an assumed family name Belinda and Daniel began their first week in what had been a picturesque resort, though now quantities of trash rendered the beach fit only for gulls and rats. The paint on their rented Volkswagen half gone, the vehicle did not standout amid the battered bicycles and mangy donkeys in the seaside town which had seen better eras.

One morning only a week after their arrival, the engine conked out on the main road. They flagged a rickety extra-large taxi and the driver offered to take them to the school. En route they picked up and dropped off more passengers.

Two new passengers suddenly gave directions to detour to a guardhouse at the border. When the taxi-driver hesitated, they reinforced their orders with a show of Berettas. Canvas bags went over the heads of both Belinda and Daniel, their hands were tied together, and they were forced to the car floor. Belinda tried to cradle Daniel with her body, but both could feel every swerve on the increasingly rough roads. Once they were pulled out of the taxi, while captors and prisoners relieved themselves in a ditch, then all were back aboard. The taxi drove through one noisy village after another between a few miles of fields and desert, then they paused at another guardhouse where the driver was dismissed and one of the new passengers took over.

Finally, the taxi stopped and the bags were removed from their heads. They were instructed to relieve themselves in the field, then pushed into the only farmhouse in sight, to descend via a trap door and down a ladder which descended into a cellar. Their captors expressed annoyance at the need to lower Daniel into a sort of hammock down the hole, and without demonstrating any extra care, did so. His wheel chair remained in some room above.

The man who seemed to be in charge shone his flashlight on a tarpaulin in a corner. His companion lowered a chamber pot, several bottles of a watery orange drink and some biscuits, then the men raised the ladder and disappeared.

The following weeks were days and nights in hell. Medieval dungeons couldn't have been worse. By day, dim light filtered down the ladder when someone lowered or tossed down slabs of flat bread, sometimes goat cheese and bottles of orange drink. A rope was lowered for the purpose, Belinda quickly understood, of tying on the chamber pot. During all their previous years of living in close quarters, they'd been discreet about bodily functions: now Belinda had to steady Daniel on the pot. Only the mice observed their activities.

No communication with the outside world, nor with their captors—quite likely Hamas supporters who spoke a Lebanese form of Arabic. Or Turks? ISIS operatives? Chechens?

Finally, a man appeared at the top of the ladder and questioned them in imperfect French as to why they were in the country. Their cover as relief teachers he dismissed. Belinda asked him to contact what was left of the French embassy in Beirut, then in Damascus, then Cairo. Though some contacts were presumably made, they got nowhere. As for a possible ransom—

"Personne vous connait, aucun pays ne veut acheter votre liberté."

Belinda had seldom asked her parents for money except for enrollment in courses, Daniel never. The final hope, they now decided, wasn't the retired Congressman Smithington who was showing signs of amnesia, but Melanie, who still had her marbles, and might realize something was very wrong.

More weeks in the cellar while negotiations continued, fruitlessly. Their captors, evidently part guerrillas, part patriots, part terrorists, took ages to find intermediaries through which to communicate the need to obtain a considerable sum of in fungible US $100 bills.

At last the ladder was slid down the opening under the trap door and a coarse male voice ordered, "Vite, vite!" They staggered from the ladder into the sunlight. A man with a checkered red-and-white bandana motioned for them to wash in the bucket lifted from the well. He handed Belinda a long cotton dress and head scarf, and Daniel a loose shirt and baggy trousers. Someone behind them lifted them none too gently into a truck carrying watermelons. Daniel's wheelchair was folded into the back. A man with a shot gun followed them aboard. The driver, whose face they never saw, turned on the ignition, the vehicle snorted and choked and turned onto a curvy, bumpy road. At one point they seemed to stop at a roadblock, and finally allowed through.

Several hours later the car stopped beyond what had sounded like a town, the driver got out, returned, gestured to them to get out and hurry to the door of a low yellow stucco house, the only house in sight. Belinda helped Daniel into his twisted wheelchair. A young man emerged and hurried them into the house.

"Come, come in! I am agronomist, friend in Peace Corps, he asked I get you to right people...You illegal, big risk for me."

"If you could get us to any American, he or she would quietly get us out of the country." Belinda and Daniel remained unsure what country. "Do you have any aspirin?"

The agronomist brought aspirin, a jug of boiled water from the little refrigerator, tomatoes and goat cheese from the counter, showed them to an outdoor shower. He insisted they sleep in his double bed while he slept on the couch in the little living room. He never asked their names nor gave his own.

Before dawn he revved up his Volkswagen and delivered them to the home of an American, a former AID worker who had married a local, sired six children, and stayed there.

Belinda and Daniel knew better than to ask for more details. "Thank you," he said. "We will forget we ever met you.

Both would forever be haunted not only by the under-cover assignment gone wickedly haywire, but as much by the dismissive words of the American chargé d'affaires to whom their host delivered them. "Sorry but we mustn't tear the fragile spider web which could rip if news of your adventure reached the press…Sorry, Mr. and Mrs. Smithington, this is a gag order…I'll get you out of the country but your presence, if reported to anyone, could also cost me my job."

Was he too nonplused to offer sympathies for their long, painful, imprisonment?

After hasty debriefings, the procuring of newly-minted passports with exit visas, then several changes of planes and countries, two sleepless days later they were in a rented car en route to the dilapidated estate….

The old lawns had grown into savannahs, and old pin oaks, evergreens and lilacs were shedding their dead branches all over the farm.

Daniel resumed playing the old grand piano, newly tuned, and since his eyesight was dimming, fortunately he had memorized a broad repertoire and his fingers on the keys had remained sure. Over the next months, however, extra notes increasingly slipped in or escaped before hearing, due in part to increasing blindness, but also, Belinda realized, to fading memory. This also meant he didn't see her wrinkles, and gallantly claimed her chunkiness gave him more to hang onto in the darkened bedroom.

Under the house, she held the flashlight while Mr. Melton reached for a wrench to tackle the drainpipe. Tomorrow she'd buy more aluminum tape, and clear the dead branches scattered around the farm. The firewood would be welcome on winter evenings.

Offspring of the county's once most notable family, they were now merely two aging cousins on a ramshackle farm.

Barbie of the Bee Port

BARBIE of the Big…Whatevers! That's what the 7-Eleven cashier called me? Guess some folks do, sometimes, behind my back. I don't like it.

My breasts *are* large, one pimply boy said, "hu-mon-gous." Maybe they do help draw clientele into this Peppermint- Stick-Look-Slick-Quick-Clip-Curl and We-Cut-All-Kinds shop: my ladies like a cushion while I'm shampooing, streaking, trimming, waving. Some men hanker for mama's mammaries.

Don't mean to shock you, Mister Outta-Towner, that's what my Marys who work nursing say.

Big chests good for singing, you say?

I sing mornings showering, when nobody around to overhear. Peter-Baby, my Coast Guard son, found '78s in Mongolimum though the storekeeper said Youkrainium, in some thrift store up the coast, our Victrola still works, I can pick up the tunes though I don't understand the words.

Something like *lubov* and *lublue* or *blublue*. This morning being warm, while airing my breasts, I sang along as if I understood.

Someday I'll tell Peter-Baby more about his daddy.

Watch that bee, Mister! Don't sit on it. *Him*, I mean, it's gotta be a worker bee and they're all males…

I only hum while shaving and shampooing my clientele.

Bobby the Sheriff calls me a "One-Woman Muzak." My clientele want to talk, be heard, not be argued with. Smiley, the sourpuss bartender by the harbor, claims I steal his business, he's Port Shrink: ships put in here, sailors load up, unload, Smiley's their audience. Or I am.

When folks got me and him who'll listen, why should they piss away money on potato-face shrinks to solve "piss-ant problems in this piss-ant half-north half-south port?" Sorry, it was Step-Dad-One who said "piss-ant," not me...Or I? Today certain folks here want their "piss-ant" problems settled. More than getting their bee houses or doorsteps repaired.

Like murder: how to. Harry's planning to murder Elmira, and I'm afraid this time he's real serious. Both my regulars, known them since Elementary. Gotta head Harry off before Bobby the Sheriff arrives, after closing time. Bobby wants Cover-the-Gray, won't say why, something undercover.

New lady from elsewhere, says her name "Jane Smith," just moved to Bee Port, starting a new job tomorrow, also wants after-hours appointment so nobody knows her "blondness needs re-blonding. Want ringlets, facial, scarlet nail polish."

Whose back she gonna scratch tonight?

Me? Nobody whose back to scratch anymore...Low on dough, too young for Medicare, house hundred years too old for repairs, but the bees find plenty of places under the shingles to nest. So like everyone else her, I got a lifetime supply of honey. Ma's Edsel she got cheap broke so I stay slim walking.

Old machinery, new machinery, I hope that new washer- dryer that Harry, in a better state a couple days ago, connected works. Laundry bag's full with Cut-n-Curl's smocks—they're peppermint-striped. All our towels and capes solid maroon so hair coloring doesn't show."

Shave and haircut, Mister Outta-Towner? Oh, you stopped in only because your cell phone dropped over a bulkhead at the harbor? Sure, that cashier saw pay phones on our walls for years. Phone company cut service, left the box for decor...My cell phone's almost dead too, gotta charge.

The postman! Someday'll be a letter from—whatever that foreign place...Today: only bills, fliers for things I can't buy, fliers for things I can't do. Fliers good for starting the fireplace, winters, though a proper bee-man has to scrape in and out the chimney first.

Hey, Mister Outtatowner! That's your bus leaving! Missed it! Next bus evening...Get coffee at 7-11—thanks, for me too.

Hanging out here's no problem. Can barber you in a while.

That Harry who is dead set on murder? He checks filling stations' underground tanks, wells, septic tanks. Hope different dipsticks. His sign reads: *YOUR HOLE IS OUR GOAL.* Today he's jumpy as a sump pump, got a book on poisons Should see a shrink.

I'd never patronize a shrink, and anyway, I don't talk much except *mmmm, uh-huh, lathering, snip you, style you,* while my customers prattle on.

"Don't gossip, talk religion or politics," Ma said, and "above all don't mess with the law."

Ma, we've got a mess for the law today.

I keep Ma up even now, Mister Outta-Towner. She had lotta wisdom younger, read cards, *knew* things. When Real-Dad passed, Ma inherited his Clip'n'Curl shop his barber pole, his debts. Later, Step-Dad-One's debts, then Step-Dad-Two's debts when he passed. Her own funeral, whole port attended.

She'd baked and frozen cookies the week before, like she *knew*...

This rose-glass bowl full of peppermint sticks? Guys come in fishy, sweaty, hungry, I give 'em a stick. Kids—

Ma had six. Six kinds of hair, I learned barbering on every one, can handle any walk-in. Siblings work Elsewhere. Me, the runt, I run Clip'n'Curl now.

Our port's not prosperous, Coast Guard base is way around the peninsula, cruise ships and yachts want them hot duty-free islands. Fishing boats, trawlers, freighters drawing shallow, they'll put in here for emergencies.

Like that foreign freighter what busted her boilers. Cold War then, people watching foreigners, illegals. Port buzzed over those wrong-side-out letters.

Big sailor walked in here, asked "Cut?" in a funny accent.

He also looked—foreign. Not quite like the cooks in the Oriental restaurant, but a bit different look to his eyes. Ma busy permanenting Elementary's principal, Step-Dad-One barbering the mayor, me, in training, 14, but my hand-me-down sweaters tight so people guessed me older. I was just done checking kids for lice, when that shabby swabby pointed to me then to his squirrel's-nest of dirty-dark hair and auburn beard. Hartz Lice Killer worked on our Hound-Dog, works on kids, worked on him. I hacketted, Hartzed, rinsed, trimmed, conditioned, then sprayed Lysol around.

"Like forest," he sniffed, handing me a sorta Monopoly dollar.

"Don't worry him about no bill," Ma whispered. "Offer peppermint sticks."

He ate three, pointed to his stomach. "Café?"

Ma invited him home for dinner: "We've never had a foreigner. I baked a cake this morning, started the stewpot."

Strewpot. Chickens, rabbits, vegetables, raccoons, whatever. I hoped no rats.

The Mongolium or whatever, from someplace in Europe or maybe the Orient, that sailor, he walked home with us, left his shoes outside, stepped in gawking like he'd never seen an American home. He petted Hound-Dog and the cats, then sniffed Ma's strewpot, kissed her hand like she was some queen.

Ma looked around. "My cake?"

"Raccoons sneaked in Hound-Dog's door—" my twin big brothers, Ted and Mike—"Tad" and "Mite" for their size—said in chorus, icing on their chins.

"No problem." That foreign sailor saw our radio's insides strewn around, fixed it, helped bolt the snowplow on the tractor. Ma who could guess things coming, she knew it'd snow, people'd need plowing out.

Step-Dad-One set out shot glasses for everyone but me, poured whiskey.

The sailor shook his head, "Must go ship or captain Gulag me."

I didn't know what "Gulag" meant, not then. Anyway, he stayed for supper. We ate Ma's strew-stew, everyone talking at once. My night to wash up, but he scrubbed the burnt pot. He noticed Real-Dad's old guitar from the wall, took it down and adjusted the strings, we got to singing—his basso hit my stomach. Explaining one foreign song meant "black eyes, like you," he toasted me, kissed my hands. Teaching each other tunes, everyone sang like no tomorrow. More shots of whiskey, last song sounded like going down the drain.

He kept saying "Must go" but fell asleep on the brown couch. Snow starting, Ma threw my other blanket over him, followed Step-Dad-One to bed. Tad and Mite had the loft, sisters' room full of sisters, my bed was the green couch opposite the brown one.

The sailor from Mongolium or wherever woke up, wanted to practice English, "I learned words from lady on TV Leningrad." He taught me foreign words, I taught him American. Furnace down nights to save money, house freezing, we doubled up, tickled, scratched, hugged and kept each other warm practicing words.

Sun-up, he jumped up, buttoned up. "I late, means Gulag for Mama—Siberia."

His shoes holey, I found Real-Dad's boots. Too big for Tad or Mike, too good for Goodwill, saved in the closet, those boots fit that Mongolium perfect.

"I bring next trip. Must quick find ship—"

I grabbed someone's pea coat, ran behind, scuffing his tracks. Hound-Dog followed, barking. Men in long coats were herding sailors, like cows, staggering up the gangplank to his freighter. I saw some of their faces, some very pale like they worked on the guts of the ship and never saw daylight, others dark like Africa or India…

The Mongolium kissed all over my face, his beard snowflaked and cold but soft. "I come back, Black-Eyes! Love you—Wait me—" The ship's whistle sounded, he leapt to the gangplank.

"Your mocs are soaked!" Ma fussed when I got home. "You'll catch pneumonia! Here's coffee… sugar…whipping cream."

My first coffee. Didn't get pneumonia, got fat.

The brown couch-cover was stained. "From Hound-Dog," I said. And it went into the washer, then on the clothesline where it froze, stayed spotted. Ma'd bought this peppermint-striped denim, so, being as Elmira and I took Home Ec together, we sewed new covers, then decorated Cut'n'Curl with leftover peppermint denim—look around!

Elmira's the wife Harry murdering. I won't say nothing to Bobby the Sheriff, but gotta do something...

How about a haircut now, Mister? Lotta time, lotta hair...No?

That special sailor who stayed? Ships dock, ships depart, nobody like him ever climbed over our bulkhead again.

I billowed like a spinnaker, not from Ma's cooking. Ma was built big, kept surprising folks by having another "gift from the Lord," a week later back at Cut'n'Curl, new baby in that playpen. I'm thin now but see those snapshots beside Ma's silk orchids? In a peppermint smock, who'd notice me different?

Step-Dad-One called me Plumpkin, pinched my fanny funny when nobody home...

Ma, bless her, didn't throw me out. She talked of her own "late-life gift from the Lord." That Saturday, Labor Day, she read my cards, handed everyone else cash for the Fair. "Day-off till midnight, kids. But don't you stop at Smiley's Bar coming home." Step-Dad One was off managing the shop and surely not remembering he wasn't supposed to stop at Smiley's.

Before sunset she delivered my "early gift from the Lord."

Ma'd borrowed *Tale of Peter Rabbit* when we raised rabbits, I learned to read with it, promised to name a someday-baby Peter, or if a girl, Mary after Ma but nicknamed Mopsy.

When he banged his big head and dragged his parafernalia outta me, I screamed "Peter!" Ma remembered that foreigner had said something sounded like "Petya," though we"d thought he meant "pet you" to the dog, but this wasn't quite right either.

Ma never let us skip school unless we showed fever, but this time sent a note with the twins: "Barbie quarantined: spots." I had honest-to-God spots—chiggers...

Everyone played with Peter-Baby, and I nursed him where nobody saw, even took him out to the barn to find privacy...

Soon my sisters were making babies, moving out and in, marry-ing, kids running around, Peter-Baby fitted in. I sang everyone to sleep. The shop and Peter-Baby kept me busy.

'Course I cried for that foreign sailor, sometimes still do when, like this morning, my head hears a tune.

"Forget tears for lost sailors," Ma said, "go have some fun. I kin babysit."

Boys invited me for dances, all we did was kiss. Bobby tried more, even proposed. He talked cop-talk like movies think real cops talk, left for Boston, cop school, back here as sheriff with tattoos, chowder accent, still sweet-talks me. I turn him down but we stay friends. He brings carryout and coffee, tells me enough things confidential, I could walk a beat. Monday said his 911 girl's left to work for an Ari-zona morgue. Dead-end job, I'd say.

"Her replacement's arriving today. Furrin name. From her photo, real looker."

He used to call me a looker…Yes, others sweet-talked me too. Now they tell me about their sweethearts— Couldn't I listen, give my penny-ante advice? How long since anyone confided love for me…

What if that freighter put into port in hot weather like today?

Like I always ask myself, when I think of it, or hear a certain tune…But I can't answer that, Mister Outta-Towner…

When I turned 25, Tad and Mite teased, "Nobody'll want an old maid!" So when Lanky-Lank bought me a ring from the Benjamin Franklin Five-and-Dime, Ma said I should say "yes."

Lanky-Lank? Greyhounded here from Oklahoma with cases of nuts-and-bolts for marine repairs. Ma rented him my moved-out sis-ters' old room. Boney-old, bald, 40, but he proposed, and Ma said, "a good man for you and Peter-Baby." Lanky-Lank figured him my kid brother, let him build towers with the bolts. Soon bang-bang-bang, we had Mary Ann, Mary Lou, Mary Sue. We'd sing out, "Mary-Mary-Mary," like calling cats, all three'd run indoors. Bobby,

Harry and Smiley—they godfathered them all at once, hard to re-member who which, especially when they all come to the house at once.

My house now. Lanky-Lank returned to Oklahoma to bury par-ents, died there too. I'd never leave here.

Holidays, everyone returns—so much laundry, broke the washer! This new washer-dryer, twenty buttons, delivered here, Monday. Be-fore Harry got crazy, he hooked it up.

Today I'll test it.

You need the MENs? Unisex, beyond the alcove Peter-Baby built.

Must not say "Peter-Baby:" he's six-foot-six. When he was only sixteen, the Unemployment Office wrote 18, tug job. Now he's Coast Guard. The Marys call him "Unck Redbeard."

Yes, several years ago I read what "Gulag" meant, and I under-stand now why the foreign sailors from wherever worry about not making it back to whatever their ship... In my bureau I discovered that Monopoly-money, cried for someone whose name I never knew. Gave the money   to Peter-Baby—kid should have something from his daddy. Peter-Baby hasn't landed anywhere he could spend it, stays in his wallet.

In home port, Peter-Baby brings mates in for haircuts, home for supper. If they don't make it to their ship, we've couches and can sleep several...Two Marys already are engaged to sailors, third Mary landed herself an engineer, and they all stay here when they're in port.

Oh, oh, my charger wasn't plugged tight!

Try stir-fry from Golden Pagoda, Mister Outta-Towner. I barber their cooks. They gave me that big bag of fortune cookies but plastic too tough to tear. My last fortune cookie read, *Every man a volume, l earn to read him.* I'm a big reader: leather-bound, clothbound, pa-perback, Internet when the Marys visit with laptops. Ma said, "You must've read that foreigner by Braille." Nicest book ever. TV-lady got it right when she said, "Cain't judge a book by its cover, but you can rewrite someone's story." Wish I could rewrite mine, or his.

Look, Harry's outside! Sitting in his pickup, reading. Didn't read much in school except comics. Not someone who'd do in the mother of his four kids. Hair like a hedgehog, escaping his ponytail. Today he's wearing his Harley-Davison tee "saved for important occasions." Murder's an occasion? Elmira hated her long corkscrews in Bee-Port Elementary, took garden shears. Now she's grown, and I'm grown, I do her better, but her style's awful mannish. "Never had trouble getting boyfriends," she says...

Time to turn my sign, lock up. Mister Outta-Towner, mustn't miss your bus again! No, only one motel in Bee- Port, and it's got roaches and rats. And bees.

That's Harry coming in now. Bobby's waiting outside in his cop car.

Harry, Honey, we close early Wednesdays...Ok, sit down on the sit-and-wait bench, read *Mind Your Motors* . Five minutes give me. Stop talking silly.

Two sailors walking in—I give 'em each a hug. I knowed these boys since their baby-curl cuts.

"One last trim before you're off to—Antarctica?" "Can't say, Miz Barbie, secret stuff."

"But we hear they got those big black-and-white birds…"

They notice the fluorescent bulb overhead flickering, three bulbs dark Bless 'em, they're dragging the ladder from the closet—They've put in all the spares! Real nice. Sailor pay low, they get buzz-cuts-and-hugs half- price…Free today. Yes, I got a soft spot for sailors.

That's Sheriff Bobby's coming in!

"Reckon it's late enough so all your clientele's gone."

Mostly he's stopping fights at Smiley's bar, driving drunk sailors back to ships, looking for illegals, giving Elmira speeding tickets. Harry thinks something else. No uniform today. But Bobby, why that big raincoat? Ain't raining. You look like those flashers cops arrest. Hang it on a hook …

I wrap him in capes. Keeps head down into old hunting monthlies, doesn't want nobody to see him getting Cover- the-Gray. Face lathered like Ma's cakes, you'd not know him. Won't say why, but he whispers again have I got any musk cologne...

Sorry, Mister Outta-Towner, Bee-Port once had an old- fashioned tourist house, but it got sold to become the doctor's office. People say I could make my big old house into a bed-and-breakfast, but I need it for when Peter- Baby and the Marys come home.

Oh, must be the new lady knocking...

...I slap a green-mud mask on her face, gooey her hair with chemicals, adjust the dryer like a helmet while her color's setting. Not switching it on yet. She hides behind movie magazines.

Harry's on the bench grumbling about poisons, but TV and radio full blast, nobody but me can hear...

And you, Mister, in the alcove—Nobody knows you anyway, or you them. If you miss—

I plunk Harry by the farthest basin. Industrial-strength horse shampoo, this bottle I keep for him. Chamomile grows beyond my tomatoes, I'll boil tea. "Here's a cup—"

"Rather a cuppa beer...Poison, slow-acting, or should I shoot him ratatatat like the cop he is?"

"Shhhh..." I wrap capes around him, pull his head back between my breasts. This usually soothes a man. "What's wrong, Honey? Elmira trashed your comics? Burned your oily tee-shirts? Make peace!"

My old Lanky-Lank was peaceful, no faults, bless him, though between us, he weren't exciting enough for faults. Nothing to look at either.

Nobody is, since that—whatever he was.

Peter-Baby got his looks—Sorta foreign, at least eyes like from somewhere else. Girls all fall for him.

I keep industrial-soaping Harry's hair while he rambles on. "Y'know Elmira's 911 calls? Tickets for speeding, parking crazy, sheriff must've written fifty. Y'know how she pays 'em off? I'm gonna kill them slow with poison, or fast with my chainsaw!"

Ma, we need to talk. Wish they had cell phones in Heaven. How'd they charge them? Don't get your panties in a bunch, you'd say. But Ma… Poor Ma—they don't sell Depends in Heaven, how d'they dispose of them?

Overboard clouds?

Thinking what she'd do, I push peppermint sticks in Harry's mouth to shut him up, and down, peppermint sticks into the other's mouths. If anyone's talking about murdering, Bobby pops him in jail for Domestic Violence.

Peppermint, Mister? No?

I've got just enough clean capes to keep everyone covered…

Drat, carry-out spilled on my smock. Lucky I keep a dress here… The new washer came with a detergent sample, I'll try it, and start the machine…

Bobby fidgets like six racehorses at one gate, turns the radio to a preacher-station, then fiddles with the dial, turns it loud enough to set the dead dancing. Hullabaloo covers everyone like the capes— Hymn's on, *Throw Out*

The Lifeline . Yes, yes…

Bobby, how can you say you're "not sure when'd Elmira have time for fooling around or getting her car nicked?" 'Course not. Four kids and her sewing business?"

"Her mom's living with us, baby-sits. Elm used to be as good a driver as you'd expect of a woman, but lately—" Both Elmira and I are as good drivers as any man, and she don't look like a woman men would fool around with—her hair buzzed short, features strong. Could be the sheriff's sister. Bobby attracted to someone who looks like him?

Harry to someone who doesn't?

Me? No one around to be attracted to…

Fine, Mister Outta-Towner, now I'll shave your five- o'clock, decent haircut, you'll be real attractive—

No?

The timer buzzes: lady's blonded enough...Gotta wash and set her. "Heaps of sexy curls?"

Most styles nowadays want blow dryers or big blue curlers but she wants the little pinks, big dryer, curling iron. I start one heating, spray her with White Shoulders, spray myself.

What if it was Harry poking his poles in the wrong places around town?

Still hot outside, air conditioners on HIGH. Must vacuum up hair—The Marys and Peter-Baby gave me this powerful vacuum.

Radio's playing *Guard the sailors tossing / On the deep blue sea...* Oh yes, yes.

Ma was sure the Mongolium or whatever sailor never drowned with his ship, he'd return someday.

"Please," Harry argues. "You've got rat poison in some cupboard."

"No, Hon. Rats keep to Pagoda. Mostly." I switch on the vacuum to drown him out, keep everyone under wraps.

Power failure!

7-Eleven's lights on... Pagoda's and the streetlamp. Only us, or we, outaged. What if the outage sparks a fire—

Should pull the fire alarm switch—but picture everyone running to the street half-shaved, half-cooked, capes flapping, curlers jiggling!

Flashlight in the clean-combs drawer...How soon before the water pump dies?

Watch for your bus, Mister—

Fuse box old, wiring old, if I pull the switch, it'll break off. Then where'd we be? Aluminum's what Real-Dad put in, end of World War Two when he could get it.. Lanky- Lank marked which fuses went for what. Ma, getting on, painted over everything.

Electricians cost... Hey Mister Outta-Towner, you understand wirings? Didn't think so...

Can't let Harry at the electricity, could get notions of electrocuting Elmira. I pour chamomile tea over his hair...towel him. Calm him...

Not Bobby and Jane Smith, both fidgety as frogs!

Got everyone colored, shampooed, rinsed, dried, combed, sprayed... "Jane Smith" fishes credit cards from her purse—Look, just like I thought: her real name's something long and Italian.

Bobby tucks cash in my pocket... hurries out... "Your raincoat, Bobby!"

All that gunshot practice, hearing's down. Under the streetlight, he meets "Jane Smith," they talk—Walk off together! Guess she's who he's meeting...

Harry, my feet ache, long past closing time. You won't find Elmira cheating on you, if she ever did...Look outside, Sheriff Bobby's off with my new lady. Go home, Harry, treat Elmira nice...Bring her Ma's silk orchids, she likes them.

Harry's hair now smells like chamomile. He hesitates, then grabs the dusty orchids, hugs me. "You maybe saved Elmira's life...Can't kill off your steady customers." He grabs his dipstick behind the door, jumps into his nicked pickup, zooms away. I slip the book on poisons in the trash. Not going to leave it out with the movie magazines...

Mister Outta-Towner, you got no time to tell me your soap-opera, I got no time to listen. Honest, though, I'm sorry to say Bye. Catch your bus but if you come through again— Okay, detour to the MEN's, if you can see to aim. Gotta close up shop, change from this dirty smock to my dress... Spray Lysol... In the dark, things can stay strewn around...Okay, sit there till the next bus...

Forget those dumb fuses, electrician'll come tomorrow, gotta call...Gotta run today's cash to bank's night slot, head home where half the lights don't work either. Nobody home also means, like this morning, enough hot water to shower, sing, dance around...

Clip'n'Curl's door's blocked by—Help, Mr. Outta Towner—a big—tramp—long gray hair dripping, gray beard. Granted we cut any sort of hair, says so on the sign.

"Sorry, closed now. Tomorrow...maybe..."

"I come now." Now he is standing here and his clothes are puddling my floor. His muddy boots—He bends over and tries to mop up but his clothes only make it wetter and dirtier. Drops a big plastic bag and stands up straight. He could use a lotta cutting. He holds out a bouquet of— dune grass, pokeweed, ragweed! "You alone in dark?"

"Husband's picking me up," I fib, pushing today's cash farther into my dress. "And the electricians. Big guys. They like a fight. Better move on fast. And my friend here—"

Damn tramp slides past me. I grab open the door— "Sheriff! Sheriff! Harry! Mister Outta-Towner! Help!" Bobby's outta sight. Harry too. Help, Mr. Outta-Towner! Forget you gotta catch your bus—

Oh Ma, what'll I—

"Don't close…please…Need cut… shave …" He sniffs the air. "Smells pine, flowers…"

Accent foreign, like I heard it somewhere. Mongolium?

He mops with his wet jacket, holds out his pick-u-li-yer bouquet… Goldenrod makes sniffles. Maroon berries shine in what light there is: Real-Dad cut pokeweed shoots when they poked through, early spring, Ma'd boil them like asparagus, but when they're grown, Poison. Foreign sailor, you know nothing on land. You'd also grab poison ivy.

Pokeweed berries scatter like blueberries across the floor. "Black Eyes, we talk—You still—"

Twenty years ago! But…I'm wary. What would Ma— "Couldn't write, only know 'Black Eyes.' Skipper makes me chief engineer, boiler room down in hold, ship pass twice far offshore between New York and Miami, skipper won't land. They say me old, but practice long swims, then two years ago, swim kilometer in Caspian Sea fastest, win prize, study English…Last night, at almost morning, moon big, we pass here, see lights, I dive, swim toward harbor. When Coast Guard searchlight, I dive, hide in little boats, swim to—America!

Reach jetty, hide, reach beach. So you take me legal. Yes?—But you have husband…"

I shake my head.

From the plastic bag, you must've swum with it on your back, you pull beat-up shoes, passports, penknife, dollars spill forth. "This time pay. This time stay, you help me get Green Card. Yes?"

How could I take you home like a stray tomcat? Haven't shopped, roof leaks, house—

He notices the burnt light bulbs. "You need me help…" Gotta help you outta your sopping clothes. My stainedpeppermint-striped smock covers you. You kin wear Bobby's raincoat for walking home. Peter-Baby clothes at home—they'd fit.

Hit that flashlight couple times, please…Can you open those fortune cookies—

I put your fist-full of weeds into the vase that held Ma's silk orchids, tear the plastic around the cookies. Like raccoons through old Hound-Dog's door, you eat every cookie but one you put in my mouth as we catch the tiny slips fluttering toward the unswept floor. I'll read your fortunes later, the sides in English. Too dark now. He points to the open fuse box. "I fix."

Tomorrow. And tomorrow gotta teach you what's good. Like the one good flower I see in the bouquet—honeysuckle. Setting you in the chair, I pull your head back, make my breasts like ear muffs, begin humming what I remember of what songs you tried to teach us, and in the flashlight's beam hack away at your hair and beard like no tomorrow.

Maybe this time you stay, maybe you don't. What other ships but breaking-down ones would put into our port?

The Big Swim

Known for winning long-distance marathons "and at her age!" this prospective journey did not raise questions other than how many times she'd be limping around the deck.

Not known was that Mrs. M. planned not to return from the trip.

But legs and ankles irreparably injured when a policeman's horse, stung by yellow jackets, ran amok as she was jogging across the park, she now navigated clutching her late father's carved walking stick. This helped her balance but merely underscored the realities of unsteadiness and pain.

So, no more running, which meant no more living to the hilt. Ergo: why bother.

Time to take action. Long a widow, no children or grandchildren, the last of her terriers given to friends on a farm, she alone was in charge of her life, and now of her—dying. Why not get it over with before the bigger limps and sharper wrinkles really set in…

She spent a dutiful eve of New Year's Eve afternoon with elderly Aunt Cynthia, who loved to reminisce about exotic travels in her youth and to give advice: "In my day, certain working ships accepted a few passengers who didn't expect room service or cocktail-hour waltzes. No tipping till the trip over…You might someday consider—"

When Mrs. M. returned to her apartment, her passport and several current statements on her desk cinched it. Her savings account held more than enough to cover a one-way ticket on a ship. She opened her laptop and Googled cruises…Damn: every ship booked until June.

An unfamiliar booking office popped up online, with a freighter, home port Sevastopol, departing New York—

Day after tomorrow!

Phoning an old lover now in real estate, she put her one- bed-room condo on the market. He blew kisses over the phone, offered to help her find new digs, and suggested a glass of champagne when she returned north, a time when his wife planned to visit aged parents in Iowa.

"Mmmm…thanks for the invitation…"

She set about paying bills, closing most accounts, donating books and CDs to the library, trophy cups to the gym, furniture, carpets, summer clothes and most winter outfits, and whatever else seemed salvageable to the Salvation Army. The crazed china and chipped glasses went into the REFUSE room, whatever was small down the chute, the rest on a shelf. To their surprise, the apartment was snapped up.

Half of the money from selling it went to refugee relief programs. Signing a check and donating excess stuff to worthy charities, she could almost believe her debts to society were paid. Enough of a tax write-off, anyway. Whatever remained on her credit card would be a waste, but her accountant, paid in advance, would wind up her financial affairs and donate the rest.

She nuked the remaining frozen crab cake in the freezer— tomorrow she would give back to the sea—and crumpled the wrappings. She stuffed her last credit card and leftover dollar bills into her purse, a swimsuit, one change of sweatpants, sweatshirt and lingerie into her backpack. Along with her parka, these should be welcomed by whoever inherited them.

Likewise her sleeping bag which she unrolled on the floor: this final night ashore, she'd sleep in her clothes and wake up ready to roll, or rather, sail.

Even in a goose-down sleeping bag, which had worked well enough on soft forest floors, the bare wood floor was unyielding. Difficult enough most nights now to fall asleep, tonight she remained awake until 3 a.m.

A snowy 5:00 a.m. when her alarm clock rang. She phoned for a taxi, pulled on her boots, rolled up her sleeping bag, strapped it atop her backpack, and picked up the walking stick. She locked the empty apartment, punched DOWN on the elevator, hung the apartment keys on the concierge's doorknob, zipped her parka, and hurried to the waiting cab. Traffic was still light.

She limped through dirty snow on the pier to a freighter with wrong-side-out letters on bow and stern. At the gangplank, a burly red-haired and red-bearded sailor glanced at her reservation and passport, and pointed to is chest. "I, Boris." He picked up her backpack but walked too quickly up the ramp for her to introduce herself. At least the deck had been shoveled though slippery in places.

The ship's captain, also burly but his hair turning gray, had the impossible surname Pschimaxwe. She caught only first names as he introduced his crew: "Viktor, he chief engineer, Vanyushka he really Ivan cook-bartender, Boris, he have other name but we say Boris, everythink else, sometime navigator. All know work everythink."

The three other passengers, perhaps bilingual but their countries-of-origin hard to fathom, were a seemingly pleasant middle-aged couple, Geogi and Galena, and a little girl, presumably theirs, with blond curls, an angelic expression, and ill-fitting clothes.

"We call her Doushenka, means little darling, though she not Russian. Cannot say what is. She talk only to cat." The captain pointed toward the bow, where the child and an Angora tabby sat in the lifeboat lashed to the foredeck.

Boris lifted the heavy hatch cover and led the way down the ship's narrow stairs—Mrs. M. must be careful!—to a cabin barely big enough for the bunk and small wardrobe. A head and shower lurked behind a flowered curtain. Too thin a blanket for January: her sleeping bag would be welcome.

"Big cabin next door," Boris said. "When we get to port in south—"

What need for a bigger cabin for only one night? The bigger cabin was anyway occupied by Georgi and—was her name Gale something? Oh…Galena…

A small porthole showed the predawn harbor, where ships looked festive with colored lights strung along their guy wires. Mrs. M. returned to the deck, and watched dockworkers loading crates and a few burlap bags from trucks to pier and onto and into the freighter. A tug chugged close, and the crew tossed thick hawsers toward the freighter's bow. The captain climbed the stairs to the deckhouse, the pair of other adults close behind. Mrs. M. would have joined them but felt she should wait until invited. Child and cat remained in the forward lifeboat, observing the scene.

Shivering, she realized that in her hurry to nab whatever passage, she'd not factored in how frigid the ocean in January, nor how ravenous she was.

A whistle shrilled. On the pier, Viktor and Igor unwound hawsers from the pilings, attached them to a waiting tug, then climbed a rope ladder to the freighter's deck. The tug began to propel the freighter toward the harbor mouth. Mysterious machinery grumbled. The men cast off the hawsers, and, dodging miniature icebergs, the freighter moved under her own power. Ocean swells began rocking the ship, icy wind made the ship screech—

Glad for her parka and walking stick, Mrs. M. gripped the rail. Boris brought a canvas deckchair and a faded flowered quilt, then returned with a plastic cup and a bottle of clear liquid. "Vodka?"

With a seemingly pan-Slavic captain and international crew, why not vodka for breakfast! "But not yet." She pointed to 19:00 hours on her watch. Boris seemed fascinated by the oversized dial with extra knobs for a stop watch, a weather app, an app to count steps. Now she knew to whom to leave it.

Boris carried the vodka up to the deckhouse, then brought two hunks of black bread and two small bottles of apple juice to Mrs. M., and beckoned to Doushenka. The child hesitated, then shyly came over, ate one slice, drank one juice, and climbed back into the life boat. The couple remained in the bridge with the captain, though the woman emerged briefly to look down, presumably to check on the child.

Tomorrow, or the next day…Strange way to greet the New Year, for whatever that was worth.

Waves or swells not too heavy, ship not rocking too much, at least yet, but later in open ocean…Ironic to get seasick… Sleep enveloped her…

Twilight when she awoke. Channel markers blinked offshore, seaside towns blinked onshore. Sea not too rough. She'd not thought to ask the booking office about their route to Sevastopol. "Shouldn't we be on open ocean by now?" she asked Captain Pschimaxwe when he passed by.

"Baltimore, Norfolk, Savannah, Miami—Ship take on— 'Scuse—" Wind swept away the rest of his words. Pulling the hatch cover up, then down after himself, he vanished below decks.

An hour later Doushenka stood struggling to open the hatch, then put both hands in a position which the world over indicates a need to pee. Grabbing her walking stick, Mrs. M. got up, lifted the hatch, and the child hurried down the stairs. The doors to the bigger staterooms, in one of which presumably the child would be sleeping, were locked. With little of value among her remaining possessions, up for grabs anyway, Mrs. M. had not bothered with the key: let anyone take whatever. She beckoned to Doushenka, who hesitated, then, raced inside, and emerged several moments later. They climbed back up the ladder, returned to the deck. "Come—"

The child patted the cat, then perched on the extension of the deck chair, and in silence they watched the graying sea and sky until Ivan beckoned them down to the galley. The cat slipped in behind them. Captain Pschimaxwe and the couple joined them at the table. He addressed Giorgi and Galena and the crew in what might be Greek, Ukrainian or maybe some ancient language from Persia. All had already enjoyed vodka.

Another bottle appeared on the table. Ivan-Vanka filled shot glasses, then more apple juice for Doushenka. "Welcome aboard!" the captain said, and began to sing in some unidentifiable language: perhaps a grace, perhaps a drinking song, perhaps both.

They toasted Mrs. M. with a "Heppi Noo Year!" and tossed off their vodkas. Ivan (she would settle for plain Ivan) refilled the glasses. She raised her glass to their inscrutable vocabularies, and sipped the clear liquid—Ouch! Her lips and tongue on fire!

The captain whispered, "Rum good in tea. Next port— Now must steer—"

Ivan brought a glass of tea and a pot of some kind of berry jam in it, then disappeared. Viktor poured juice for Doushenka, then ladled out a reddish stew—borscht? The child was having trouble cutting the large chunks of beef. Since the couple, presumably her parents, were preoccupied conversing with the captain, Mrs. M. sliced the child's meat into smaller pieces. She slipped bits from her own bowl to the ship's cat—how to make a friend-for-life. At least for what remained of her own.

Already 9 p.m., dark and cold. The younger man lifted the hatch cover, put his arm around the shoulders of his now- unsteady wife (?) and helped her down the ladder to their cabin. Mrs. M. had occasionally disappeared with her late husband, or several lovers along the way, and yearned for their warmth.

"Come, Doushenka," Viktor opened the hatch and led the little girl below. Mrs. M., increasingly sleepy, followed. She noticed their going not into the cabin with the couple, but into the captain's cabin. In the moment before the door closed, she spied a small hammock suspended on the far side, and soon heard Viktor singing what surely was a lullaby.

She went into her cabin and, still dressed, curled up on the bunk and spread the sleeping bag around herself.

*

Already 9:00 a.m.! She stripped and showered, washing yesterday's clothes. Wondering why she was bothering, she hung them dripping on the shower handles, dried herself with the thin towel, and reached for her other set of clothes.

Damn! Her passport, still in the pocket of her freshly washed sweatpants, was soaked, the ink of old signatures smearing. Double-damn, but no matter. At least her remaining credit card was plastic. She pulled on her dry set of clothes and jacket, climbed the stairs to the deck, and with that she hoped was a grand enough gesture, tossed her passport over the port side toward the blurry sunrise. She started back down the stairs.

The heavy door to the galley opened and Ivan beckoned her in and pulled out a chair between Boris and Doushenka. Ivan set down a plastic plate with two fried eggs leering up. She was accustomed to morning workouts, fruit for breakfast, and never ate anything fried. "Thank you for the eggs," she nonetheless said.

"Eggs?" Ivan repeated but didn't offer an equivalent in whatever mother tongue.

"Eggs…Fork, please?" Mrs. M. tried next, "Spoon."

Ivan and the child both repeated, "Fork, spoon." This might provide entertainment until the ship headed farther out to sea, so she went on. "Fork…knife…milk…"

"Milk…fork…knife…" they repeated. Boris asked, "What this?"

"Plate, or dish," Mrs. M. said.

"Plater dish," they repeated.

"Vodka!" The captain seized a bottle from a cupboard and headed out.

*

The freighter was still following the East Coast southward, gulls whitening the deck, the crew hosing and scrubbing. Daily Boris asked Mrs. M. for a word or whole sentence, and wrote it down. Sometimes a beef stew appeared at the galley table, but whenever the seas were calmer, Viktor cast a line and pulled in a fish of a not always recognizable species. All of Igor's mysterious soups tasted delicious.

Doushenka and the cat now seldom left her side.

At the port of Baltimore the captain, flashing a passport too quickly for her to make out whatever country-of-origin, disembarked with an empty shopping cart. The Immigration officer accepted Mrs. M.'s explanation that the wallet with her documents had fallen over-

board. "Sorry, lady, though I guess you need to exercise your legs…
But stay right on this here pier and use your cane against the rats."

Two hours later the captain returned with his shopping cart full
of bags of potatoes, beets, cabbages and unidentifiable meat. Reach-
ing the bottom, he retrieved several bottles. "Vodka! Red wine! Rum!"

The weather progressively warmer, like the others, Mrs. M. shed
her jacket, and took her frequent limps around the deck in progressively lighter clothes. The freighter docked in Norfolk and Savannah,
and headed toward Jacksonville. Captain Pshmim, Viktor and Ivan
took turns going ashore. Doushenka, Boris, Mrs. M. and the pair of
other adults, all presumably without proper documents, remained
aboard. Mrs.

M. occasionally wired her accountant to transfer money to Captain Pshmim's account, until only a few dollars remained. She pan-
icked.

"No worry," said Captain Pshmin. "You teach us English."

In Miami, she asked the immigration officer if she could find the
dollar store a tattered guidebook said was across the nearby park. "I
need to walk—"

"Ok, but I'll keep an eye on you. Stay in sight. Be back in a ten
minutes."

She quickly bought crayons, blank paper, two size 6 and two size
12 tee-shirts and shorts, a size 6 bathing suit, and small and medium
large flip flops. Doushenka took off her scuffed shoes, and Mrs. M.
was alarmed to see many scars on the child's feet.

Both wearing their new shirts and shorts, they stretched their legs
in the sun, opened the crayons and began drawing ships.

Captain Pschmim paused to look at the pictures, and noticed the
bruises covering Mrs. M.'s legs. He disappeared, reappearing with a
jar in which swam—M'God, leeches! Before she could stop him, he
knelt at her feet and, to her horror, laid four wiggly black creatures
on her legs, where they bit her skin, began drinking her blood—

The captain applied the leeches over the next week, and to her surprise, pains and bruises gradually diminished. She also realized how—she dared not find the word—how it felt to have a man's hands on her again...

*

Sunset while they were leaving the port of Miami. Mrs. M. sat back in the deckchair and watched the half-moon appear.

When they passed the final buoy, she observed Boris in bathing trunks and tee-shirt slip overboard. He began to swim toward land. A small knapsack in a plastic bag bobbed on his back.

Struggling to her feet, she was about to shout "Help! Man overboard!" Yet obviously he had prepared for this: far be it for her to interfere. And he seemed to be a strong swimmer. She settled back as he vanished from sight, and prayed for his safe landing on whatever beach.

Tomorrow, or the day after, she too, but not toward land—

In the morning, the ship-to-shore radio led off with the news that a sailor, apparently Russian, Ukrainian, some sort of

Slav anyway, jumped overboard, swam to a beach south of Miami, changed to dry clothes, walked to town, found a police station, and asked for asylum. Immigration officials arrived and quizzed him. He spoke enough English, which Mrs. M. realized she had unwittingly helped him learn, to plead his case. Calls to Washington resulted in a US State Department officer with limited Russian flying to Miami, but it was far from certain that Boris would be allowed to stay. He remained in the county police station, and the Coast Guard escorted the freighter back to port. Officials and journalists flocked, tablets and cell phones open...

...Even when the event ceased to be newsworthy, Miami police ordered the freighter to remain in port while the problem was resolved. This delay, however, would give Mrs. M. time to locate an immigration lawyer to take on the child's case—

Before she could find a Miami phone directory, Captain Pschimaxwe grabbed her hand to accompany him to the police station and translate—"But careful," he whispered, "you not legal!"

In the end it was she who persuaded Boris to get back aboard and the Immigration officials to agree that he was essential to the freighter's operation, no charges would be leveled or reports sent home. Wherever home was. Back aboard, Boris hesitated, then hugged the captain, Victor and Ivan. Mrs. M. unstrapped her wrist watch and presented it to him. Boris bent over and kissed her hand. Doushenka hugged his knees, and he lifted her onto his shoulders for a pony ride around the deck.

Mrs. M. would have liked to hug the whole lot of them,.

She also realized that all morning, her walking stick had remained in her cabin…

The freighter got underway, heading ever southward. Docked in Rio, Mrs. M., watched Giogi and Galena, whose surnames she never learned, disembark with their luggage, show whatever documents to a uniformed official, and disappear into the crowd.

The freighter continued through the Caribbean, pausing at other ports. When open water seemed clean, the crew lowered a ladder, and everyone took a dip. Mrs. M. taught Doushenka to swim, and soon everyone was cavorting like the dolphins around them.

Ivan produced cold soups of cabbage, beets, or fish.

Captain Pschim was drinking less vodka, sometimes joining Mrs. M. with rum in tea, still always hot. Boris cleaned up the slightly-larger cabin for Mrs. M. Doushenka indicated she wanted the smaller one. Daily the captain, crew and the child learned another English word, if never enough to tell anything about themselves. Sometimes the past is better untold?

Nobody asked Mrs. M. about her own past, or was aware she had a certain reputation as a runner, in fact had won marathons. She did not enlighten them.

*

The freighter docked in Santos, Vitória, Paranaguá, then Rio. Mrs. M. and Doushenka stood at the rail watching dockworkers load crates aboard. Brazil was indeed a land of immigrants: the men were speaking not Portuguese or Spanish, but a language unfamiliar to Mrs. M. Suddenly Doushenka began jumping around and calling down to them in the same tongue. The men looked up.

"What is the child is saying?" Mrs. M. quickly asked.

Over the next half-hour, in halting English they began to interpret the confusing story...

Although her birthplace remained a mystery, she was living with an older lady who said to call her Granny on a little farm in southern Albania while her parents were working in Tirana. A bus stopped on the highway beyond the garden fence. A dozen tawny young migrants from some unidentified Middle Eastern city descended, set up camp outside the garden fence, fell to their knees and folded their hands in prayer.

Noticing strange-looking crosses around the necks of several boys, the "grandmother" brought the priest from her church to question them. He could not understand their explanations beyond the fact that they were Copts from Egypt.

Doushenka helped her "granny" bring them black bread and soup made with vegetables from the garden, and pointed out the pump and outhouse. She was fascinated by their cell phones, which she learned to recharge in the house. She brought out a striped ball and her few books, and pointing to the pictures, spoke the words in Albanian. They answered in their strange language, and remained for several days.

"Granny" had gone to the village to sell a basketful of cabbages when a large van stopped outside. The driver and a policeman began to direct the eager migrants aboard.

Doushenka went outside the gate to wave goodbye and tossed the ball up as a gift. After the last boy climbed aboard, the policeman lifted the child up and, despite her protests, loaded her in and immediately locked the rear doors. She screamed and burst into tears. The boys tried to calm her, while the truck jolted from the bumpy dirt lane onto a paved road full of potholes, then a smoother main route.

After several hours, the driver left them off by a field full of tents and large shipping cartons which served as living quarters for a number of families. Teen-agers, mostly boys, were camped in clusters. An English-speaking woman inspected the new arrivals' documents, and the boys who spoke some English interpreted for the rest. Pointing to Doushenka, who didn't resemble the tawnier migrants and lacked any common language, the woman asked for her particulars. The boys could say only that she joined them in Albania. "She now little sister."

Doushenka understood the need to give her name, finally said "Dashurie" but could not say whether name or surname.

A loudspeaker broadcast a chant. Most of the boys in the camp fell to their knees and bowed their foreheads to the ground. The dozen from the bus did not. Prayers over, the woman pointed out kitchen wagons, water jugs, portable toilets and shower stalls. She assigned the dozen Coptic boys to a large tent where many boys were already living, then beckoned the dazed child to a smaller tent where some dozen teen-aged girls had claimed the cots but tossed Doushenka a blanket…

All week the boys who'd camped outside the grandmother's garden spent hours on their cell phones, lined up for meals and showers, and sometimes tossed the ball Doushenka had given them. Then, after several scuffles with boys from other North African countries, the dozen boys adjusted their backpacks, and headed across the field toward a grove of trees. Doushenka scrambled to her feet and followed. She had trouble keeping up, but the boys paused, and took turns letting her ride on their shoulders.

After three days they reached a small port, apparently on the Croatian coast, and a freighter tied to the pier. The boys who spoke some English explained to the skipper that they were fleeing north to his uncle in England. "Please take to port with trucks or trains heading north."

When the captain demurred. "Too many…Marine police

say—" the boy said, "We clean hull." Grabbing the heavy brushes and scrapers the boys, followed by Doushenka, jumped overboard, scrubbed barnacles from the hull, and washed their clothes.

"Okay," the captain finally said, "I take you two ports north, but hope no police—"

While their clothes dried on the railings and on them, they explored the freighter. In the galley, the cook offered black bread and jam. Seeing Doushenka yawning, he pointed to a long seat cushion with a dry towel on it. Lulled by the waves, she fell asleep, not waking when the cook and the boys disembarked at another port. The cook returned after the engines began to turn, and the hawsers were thrown back aboard, then the freighter turned southeast along the coast.

*

The Brazilian foreman shouted to the Albanian dock workers: their truck leaving. The freighter also prepared to depart, and this ended the tangled attempts at explanation.

*

The child still couldn't explain who she was or why she was there.

"So she stay," Captain Pschim said. "When reach Montreal, Brooklyn, Havre—"

In every port, however, though immigration officers promised help with papers, only the captain, Viktor and Igor were allowed beyond the waterfront.

Even if allowed to immigrate, where would the child go but to some orphanage?

For the first time putting his arms around Mrs. M., the Captain led her up the steps to the deckhouse. Doushenka and the cat followed. The whistle shrilled. The freighter continued on southward, stopping in one port to load containers, at another to unload.

The End

Joan of Arc
Material: Ceramic
Size: 10H x 10W x 12D

LIST OF IMAGES

ABOUT THE AUTHOR

Elisavietta Ritchie's prose, poetry, photographs and translations are widely published and anthologized in the United States and abroad. Credits include *The New York Times, Washington Post, Poetry, American Scholar, Christian Science Monitor, JAMA: Journal of the American Medical Association, Canadian Woman Studies, Confrontation, Potomac Review,* and numerous other publications. Her translations from French, Russian, Modern Greek and Malay-Indonesian are in print, and own work has been translated into a half-dozen languages.

Tightening the Circle Over Eel Country won the Great Lakes Colleges Association's "New Writer's Award for Best First Book of Poetry, 1975-1976." Individual poems and stories won significant awards from the Poetry Society of America, National Endowment for the Arts, *The Ledge* , Bright Hill Press, and others. Several were nominated for the Pushcart Prize.

Ritchie writes, translates, edits, gives readings, workshops, serves as poet-in-the-schools, and helps writers of various ages. She was long active with the Washington Writers' Publishing House, where, after winning annual awards for a book of poetry and later of fiction, she served first as president of the poetry, then of the fiction division. She created The Wineberry Press to publish others' manuscripts too unconventional for regular presses.

She traveled to several continents independently and as a Visiting Overseas Speaker for the United States Information Service.

Her recent collection of poetry, from Poets' Choice Publishers, is *REFLETIONS: POEMS ON PAINTINGS, A POET'S GALLERY.* Readings of these poems can be accompanied with the paintings (most of which are at The National Gallery) which inspired them on PowerPoint.

For years Elisavietta Ritchie and her husband Clyde Farnsworth have been nurturing poets, writers, painters, musicians and wildlife on both shores of the Patuxent River, Maryland, the Potomac, Washington DC, and rivers and seacoasts of Cyprus, Malaysia, the Balkans, Australia, Canada, and briefly, the USSR and the African continent.

ABOUT THE SCULPTOR

Serena Bates is an established artist with a long list of accomplishments. She is an elected member of Salmagundi Club, the Mystic Museum of Art, the National Sculpture Society, the Society of CT Sculptors, the CT Academy of Fine Artists, and the Lyme Art Association. She is also an elected member of and served on the Board of Directors for the Catherine Lorillard Wolf Art Club, the oldest women's art club in the nation.

Having work in collections around the world including England, Canada, and across the United States, Serena is well known in local and national circles. Mystic Marriot Hotel, CT, features Serena's "Beached Whale Fountain" as the centerpiece of their main entrance courtyard. Stand Up for Animals prominently displays "Zhen Zhen", the beautiful bronze cat outside the entrance to the Westerly Animal Shelter, RI, and the Westerly Animal Hospital, RI, features one of her sea lions prominently at their entrance. Pleasant View Inn, RI, displays her majestic life-sized sculpture "Stellar Expectations" in the main dining gallery, while her commemorative bust of "Lennie

Colucci" sits atop the bar at The Andrea, RI, where he enjoys count-less photo-ops with patrons.

As a sculptor, Serena has won many awards, recognitions, and honors during her career, from the National Arts Club, the Salma-gundi Club, Society of CT Sculptors, the Catherine Lorillard Wolfe Club, the Academic Artist Association, Mystic Museum of Art, and the Alexy von Schlippe Gallery at the University of Connecticut, to name only a few.

Serena describes herself as a story teller. She is a representational artist with an affinity for portraits and animals, working in clay, bronze, and stone. Being non-traditional in her approach, she usually does not take measurements, but instead relies on her eye and sense of observation to interpret a subject. This approach produces what she calls a "wabi-sabi" affect, a Japanese term that literally means the beauty found in imperfection or "imperfectly perfect."

She began her journey studying at the Lyme Academy College of Fine Arts and the Rhode Island School of Design. There she stud-ied with renowned sculptors Elizabeth Gordon Chandler, Don Gale, Laci Degerenday as well as classical painting and drawing with Aaron Shikler, Dean Keller and Dan Gheno. She furthered her studies with an internship at the Kane Sculpture Studio and Foundry where she learned the process of lost wax casting. Presently Serena is furthering her education in learning the art of ceramic sculpture.

CPSIA information can be obtained
at www.ICGtesting.com
Printed in the USA
BVHW091024011118
531806BV00001B/1/P

9 780997 262995